USA TODAY & WALL STREET JOURNAL BESTSELLING AUTHOR

BECCA STEELE

Ignited

Copyright © 2024 by Becca Steele

All rights reserved. No part of this book may be reproduced or transmitted in any form or by any means, electronic or mechanical, including photocopying, recording or by any information storage and retrieval system, without written permission from the author, except for the use of brief quotations in a book review.

Editing by One Love Editing

Proofreading by Rumi

Cover photography by Wander Aguiar

Becca Steele

www.authorbeccasteele.com

This is a work of fiction. Names, characters, businesses, places, events, locales, and incidents are either the products of the author's imagination or used in a fictitious manner. Any resemblance to actual persons, living or dead, or actual events is purely coincidental.

AUTHOR'S NOTE

The author is British, and this story contains British English spellings and phrases. The football briefly referred to in this story is known as soccer in some countries.

Enjoy!

For Amy S

It was only a sunny smile,
    And little it cost in the giving;
    But it scattered the night
    Like morning light,
    And made the day worth living.

UNKNOWN

KILLIAN
PROLOGUE

His skin shimmered and sparkled with gold in the sweeping club lights, the defined contours of his body curving and flexing with effortless ease. With a graceful leap, he flipped, hooking one leg around the upper part of the pole while his fingers curled around the smooth metal surface below. As he held himself in place, upside down, a smile curved over his lips. Even though I was away from his line of sight, reclining against the soft leather of the booth in a darkened corner of the room, it felt as if his smile was directed at me.

He was captivating. Beautiful. Otherworldly.

Young.

A shadow moved in front of me, blocking my view of the dancer, and the spell was broken. "Hey, Kill. Birthday shots for the birthday boy." I blinked, lifting my gaze to see Gage grinning down at me, a tray of shots balanced on one palm—a throwback to his bartending days.

I shook my head at my colleague and friend. "My birthday was last week, and I'm too old for shots."

"Nah, you're too grumpy. Thirty is not anywhere near old, mate. You're younger than Stuart, and you haven't even reached the prime of your life, so don't even start. We came here to have fun, and we're going to enjoy ourselves, whether you like it or not." Placing the tray down on the table, he snatched up one of the shots, tipping it to his lips. "Cheers."

"If your students could see you now," I muttered, grimacing as I downed my own drink—something sour and unidentifiable that set my teeth on edge.

"Please, as if they care. They're adults themselves. They know what we get up to." He paused, smirking at me. "Okay. Maybe not you. We're all aware of your uptight asshole reputation, Dr. Wilder."

"Fuck off." Rubbing at my temples, I willed away my headache. The music wasn't helping, a steady, low throb that seemed to be timed to exactly match the pounding in my head.

Gage moved, and I was vaguely aware of him sinking down next to me and saying something to Stuart, our other companion, but my attention was once again stolen by the dancer.

As I watched, he gracefully dropped to the floor, holding himself on his toes in a balletic movement, before he spun around, holding out his hand. A stunning woman with long, shining red hair strutted onstage, taking the dancer's hand and letting him twirl her around. They were both clad in gold, matching the glitter on their skin, both beautiful and untouchable.

"That's what I'm talking about." Stuart's gaze flicked

over the body of the new dancer, his pupils dilating as he drank her in.

"Yeah," Gage agreed, giving me an inscrutable look before he returned his attention to the newcomer. "Just as hot as that blonde woman earlier, not that Kill was paying attention."

Did he know? Had he noticed that I'd been unable to tear my eyes away from the male dancer on the pole? He'd caught my attention the second we'd stepped into this area in the VIP section of Sanctuary. Even standing by the bar, all the way over the other side of the room from the table where he'd been pouring glasses of champagne, I'd found him impossible to ignore. Waves of rich brown hair, threaded with reds and golds, the colour of autumn, beautiful blue eyes rimmed with black liner, long lashes, and beautifully plush pink lips that contrasted perfectly with the defined lines of his jaw, his nose, his cheekbones. His strong dancer's body was chiselled and defined like one of Michelangelo's sculptures. Breathtaking.

I exhaled a heavy breath, wrenching my gaze away from the stage. As a principal business lecturer at London Southwark University, one of the UK's most well-respected higher education centres, I couldn't afford to let myself become distracted by beautiful men, especially not when they looked young enough to be one of my students. All that existed in my life was work. And the occasional night out that Gage or Stuart forced me to join.

Such as tonight. They'd insisted that my birthday should be celebrated, and thanks to Gage's connections, we were here, in the VIP area of Sanctuary, an exclusive nightclub in London—a place I'd never have chosen to come to if it had been up to me. The one upside was that it was likely far too expensive and far too exclusive for my students to be attending, particularly the VIP section.

Besides, this man was untouchable, regardless. He was an employee of this establishment, and even if that wasn't the case—

"Happy birthday." Gage interrupted my musings with a wide grin that instantly set me on edge. "We got you a gift."

"What gift?" I said slowly. He nudged me in the side, and I glanced up to find one of the dancers who had been onstage earlier tonight standing in front of me, holding out her hand. She was absolutely stunning, with cascades of blonde hair, full breasts, and a gorgeous hourglass figure. I'd always been attracted to both men and women, but I tended to swing more towards women, so the sight of her should have been enough to pique my interest.

Unfortunately, my mind was fixated on another dancer.

"I hear that birthday celebrations are in order." The woman smiled at me. "If you'd like to come with me…"

"What did you do?" I growled at Gage, and he held up his hands.

"Don't give me that look. You'll be thanking me in a minute. We got you a private dance with the lovely Honey Rose here."

The woman, *Honey Rose*, gave me an even brighter smile. With a glare at Gage and Stuart, I followed her out of the booth. My jaw clenched as calls of "Don't be so boring" and "Lighten up, you need some fun in your life" followed me. It wasn't that I was against private dances…for other people. For me, no. The one experience I'd had years ago had been extremely awkward and uncomfortable, and I wasn't keen on a repeat.

When we were out of earshot and view of Gage and Stuart, Honey Rose turned to me. "If this is something you don't want to do, no one is forcing you. You don't even have to let your friends know."

"Was I that obvious?"

She arched a brow, huffing out a laugh. "To me, yes. I'm incredibly good at reading people, and I could immediately sense how uncomfortable you were."

I sighed, pinching my brow. "Look. It's not you. It's—"

"You don't owe me an explanation." She studied me for a moment, a thoughtful expression on her face. "I might have an idea if you're prepared to keep an open mind. I think you'll like it."

Making snap decisions had never been my style, but Gage's and Stuart's words echoed through my mind. *Don't be so boring. Lighten up. You need some fun in your life.*

Gritting my teeth, I gave her a curt nod, and she beamed. "Great. Come with me."

Seated in a smaller version of the plush leather booth I'd been reclined in a moment ago, only without the table, I adjusted the cuffs of my shirt to give me something to do while I waited for whatever was coming next. Honey Rose had shown me into this small, mirrored room, with a booth on one side and a single chair in the centre. She'd then left me alone.

The dim, recessed lighting around the edges of the room winked out, and the sound of my rapid breathing filled the space.

Before I had a chance to process the sudden darkness,

music began playing, a low, sultry beat. My head pounded. Fuck this. I wasn't going to sit here in the dark, waiting for whatever it was.

I climbed to my feet and took a step towards where I knew the door to be.

"Wait." A hand pressed against my chest. "Sit down."

The voice was a smooth, distinctly masculine purr, and it sent a fucking shiver down my spine. I ignored it, threading steel through my tone. "What's going on? If this is someone's idea of a joke, it needs to stop right now. Turn the lights back on, this instant."

The pressure on my chest increased, and caught off guard, I took an involuntary step back. "So demanding. Why don't you relax? It seems like you need it."

"What?" I hissed.

"You heard me." The hand on my chest pushed again, and I allowed myself to be driven back into the booth. That voice...

"Good." I felt a shift in the air and then a soft huff of breath against my ear. "There's one rule you need to be aware of. One very important, unbreakable rule." Another breath, and then the presence moved, enough to create some breathing room. "Remember it. No touching the dancers."

At those words, the lights flicked back on, dimly illuminating the room.

My heart fucking stopped.

JJ

The man stared at me, those ice-blue eyes wide. Fuck, he was hot. A sexy-as-fuck man, probably in his late twenties or early thirties—my preferred age range—he'd caught my eye from the second he'd walked into my place of work. I'd noticed him looking at me, too. Those heated glances he was shooting me from beneath his thick lashes had been enough to make my dick throb, and only the knowledge that I was onstage and in full view of my employers kept me from reacting. He'd forced his gaze away from me for a moment before it inevitably returned. Then, when Honey Rose had pulled me aside and told me she'd *also* noticed his eyes on me, and he was waiting in one of the private dance rooms...I couldn't pass up the opportunity.

Now, as I drank him in, I noticed his deep brown hair—short but the perfect length to run my hand through—and his strong jawline, dusted with dark stubble. The sleeves of his midnight-blue shirt were rolled up, exposing his powerful-looking arms and those delicious big fucking hands with long, capable fingers that I wanted— No. Never mind what I wanted. The glimpses of his body that his tight shirt and fitted black trousers were giving me spoke of someone who worked out, someone who could pin me down and have his way with me, someone who was packing—

Fucking stop, JJ. You're here to do a job.

Getting a hard-on at my place of work was not on my to-do list, and it was never usually a problem. In fact, I rarely even had a chance to do a private dance. This wasn't a gay club, and it was generally the women who were requested for private dances. Having said that...since my boss, Austin, had allowed me to start dancing on the pole, my dance requests had increased somewhat, although they were usually out in the booths in the main area rather than in one of the private rooms. And no one that had requested me had ever been my type before. Not even close.

But this man...he was *so* my type. In every single way.

"You," he ground out, his fists clenching and unclenching at his sides, making the tendons of his forearms stand out in sharp relief.

With a fast, fluid movement, I swung my thigh over his, straddling him without actually touching any part of his body. I ran a hand down my chest, sucking in a breath when I saw the way his pupils dilated as he followed the path of my hand. "I saw you watching me."

His whole demeanour seemed to change at my words, his shock replaced by something else, a dark amusement that, *fucking hell*, made my dick stir despite all my warnings to myself. "For you to notice that, you must have been watching me."

I rolled my hips down, enjoying his hitched breath. All I was wearing was a pair of tight gold booty shorts, and he would soon be aware of the effect he had on me, but I found I didn't care. There were cameras in this room, but they were behind me, and as long as he remembered the rules and didn't touch me, we wouldn't be disturbed.

"You're rather noticeable," he murmured softly, almost under his breath, and I smiled. I knew and enjoyed the effect I had on men, but having someone like him notice me was incredibly flattering. Despite his tense posture and his obvious reluctance at being here—not just in this room with me but in the club in general—I'd stolen his attention. And I was greedy and selfish when it came to having the attention of a man I wanted, and so I was going to do everything in my power to make sure he remembered me long after tonight.

"Mmm. So are you." I spun around on his lap, letting my head fall back against his shoulder as I arched my back, grinding my ass down. It took every single bit of my professionalism not to react to the feel of his swelling erection against me. I'd been right—he was packing. Fuck. Some of my friends liked to call me a size queen, and maybe that was true because the thought of this big dick pounding into me—

Fuck. *Professional.* I was a fucking professional.

Planting my feet on the floor, I straightened up, sashaying away from him, and only when I was seated on the chair in the centre of the room did I dare to face him again. I closed my legs and then placed my hands on my knees, pulling my thighs apart, noticing how his dark gaze went straight to the bulge between my legs.

"Like what you see?" How my voice had managed to come out steady, I had no idea. I never even talked during dances, so this was already a new experience, and with the way this man was more or less incinerating me with his gaze... My cock hardened even further, reacting to the heat in his eyes.

He remained silent, but now he was clasping the edges of the booth seat, white-knuckling them as if it was the only thing stopping him from launching himself at me. Maybe it was. The thought of him losing control…

For the first time, I wished there were no cameras. Nothing to stop us from taking what we both clearly wanted.

"Come here," he growled, and oh, fuck, that rasp was so sexy. I shuddered despite myself, despite my professionalism—no. Who was I kidding? There was no professionalism left here.

Cameras, I mouthed, and his jaw tightened. My legs were shaky as I lifted myself from the chair, prowling back towards him and dropping down, running my hands up his tense legs all the way to the top, my gaze flicking down to the obvious tent in his trousers. As I rolled my body up, I made a decision that I never, ever should have made. One that could put my job in jeopardy, but I was too far gone to stop.

"If you want more, come to the employee door next to the bar in two minutes. It's the black one with the keypad," I whispered before darting my tongue out to taste his skin— salty and delicious.

Then, I forced myself to step away until I was outside the door of the private room, and I could finally breathe again.

Was he going to take me up on my offer? There was a huge risk to both of us—more so me than him, but this could get him barred from Sanctuary, and my boss, Austin De Witt, was someone you didn't want to cross, either.

It didn't stop me from hitting the panel that led to the employee corridor and making my way as quickly as I could down the passageway to the other door that led back out into the club, where I'd told him to wait.

When I inched the door open, my breath caught in my throat. He was there, dark desire in his eyes and no hesitation at all as he shouldered his way inside, crowding me up against the wall. Height-wise, he only had a few inches on me, but it felt as if his entire body was covering mine as he pressed into me.

"Tell me there are no cameras in here," he rasped, and I immediately shook my head, even though I didn't know for sure. Wrapping my fingers around his wrist, I dragged him down the corridor to the closest place I knew we wouldn't be disturbed—my corner of the dancers' dressing room, which was nicknamed "The Glamoriser." A heavy curtain was all that separated it from the main section with the mirrors, outfits, and makeup, and there wasn't much to it—just three walls and a wooden bench seat with the curtain across the front. But if both of us could stay quiet, we wouldn't be caught.

"If anyone comes in, don't say a word," I breathed, as he yanked the curtain shut and then crowded me back up against the wall, this time with my front pressed against the smooth surface, the heat of his body covering my back.

His head lowered to my ear, his lips skimming over the lobe. "What do you want?"

"Whatever you want to give me."

"I want to give you so many fucking things." He shifted against me, grinding his erect cock against my ass, and I moaned.

"I want you to fuck me with your big dick."

"Lube and condoms?" His voice was so hoarse.

"Yeah. Just a second." Bending at the waist, I reached under the bench seat for my bag, feeling around in the pocket where I kept my supplies. Straightening up again, I reached back, pressing them into his hands.

There was a second of silence, and then I felt his fingers curl around the packets as he dipped his head back to my ear. "You're so fucking flexible."

"Mmm. I am. You should see me suck my own dick."

A strangled sound came from behind me, and then his entire body weight was pressing into my back. "Fuck. You're driving me insane."

"Likewise. Fuck me now, please."

He muttered to himself, and above the distinctive sound of a zipper opening, followed by the tear of the condom and lube packets, I heard him say, "I never do this."

My cock and my ego swelled at the thought that I was the one to break through his boundaries. Maybe he was one of those repressed "straight" men who liked to get off with a man and then go home to their wives and pretend nothing had ever happened—but no. He hadn't seemed like that. Just...tense and kind of uptight in general. Whatever. The fact was, he was here, and his—

Oh. Without any warning, my shorts were yanked down, and a big palm was settling between my shoulder blades, applying pressure until I bowed forwards. Stepping out of my shorts, I widened my legs, arching my back, and I was rewarded with a sharp intake of breath.

Then, a finger circled my hole, coated with a generous amount of lube, and pushed inside.

"More," I commanded. "I need your cock inside me."

A low chuckle came from behind me, another finger

pressing inside to join the first, pumping in and out in a slow, lazy movement. "More already? Such a little cockslut, aren't you?"

"Yes."

The chuckle sounded again, this time slightly disbelieving, and a hand slid up my torso, over my chest, and onto my throat. "This is fucking madness. I shouldn't be here. I shouldn't be doing this. But I can't stop."

"Leave your mark on me. I want a necklace." My hand stretched up to cover his, squeezing, and he got the hint. His fingertips closed around my throat, taking care to apply pressure only where it was safe, and that level of care made my dick throb and leak even more.

"Another?" he questioned, already pressing a third finger inside, circling all three digits and opening me up, purposely avoiding my prostate as he did so. This fucking man knew exactly what he was doing.

Definitely not straight.

I needed him. Right fucking now. Rocking back on his fingers, I arched my back even further, thrusting my ass out. "Give me your cock. I want to feel you tomorrow."

"Fuck." Releasing my throat, he planted one hand on the wall, and the other gripped my hip. I felt the head of his cock at my entrance, and then he pushed inside in one long thrust.

We both moaned at the feeling. He was the perfect size for me in every way, stretching me out, making me feel so fucking full, a pleasurable burn that I knew I'd still feel tomorrow.

A soft kiss was placed on the back of my neck, right at the top of my spine, and I froze for a second before it was followed by the scrape of teeth and then a delicious rumble against my skin.

"Hold on. I'm going to wreck your pretty hole."

Yes. This was exactly what I wanted. I planted my palms on the wall, thrusting back again, and he took the hint.

His thick length drew almost all the way out, then slid back into me. Then again, and again, his movements getting faster and harder until I was moaning and writhing on his cock, my dick so fucking hard and leaking, making a mess all down my length and onto the floor.

I wanted to touch myself. I wanted him to touch me. But fuck, he was nailing my prostate, and I knew I could probably come from this alone.

"Don't stop," I panted.

"Not...stopping..." he ground out, thrusting even harder, sending me rocking forwards, my arms bracing against the wall to hold me in place as he impaled me, balls-deep, filling me so full that I couldn't even breathe. I gasped, right on a knife edge, and then his teeth sank into my shoulder as he released my hip, his fingers wrapping around my cock.

I came. Instantly. Hot pulses of cum soaking his hand and the wall and the floor, my entire fucking body trembling as he pounded me even harder, coming inside me with a choked-out moan against my skin. It went on and on, and by the time I collapsed against the wall, completely wrung out, I wasn't the only one trembling and trying to catch their breath.

His large hand came around my waist, pulling me back into him as his mouth found the side of my throat. "You're so fucking sexy," he murmured, kissing up my neck and onto my jaw. "Fuck. You don't even know how much I needed that."

"I've never done this at work before," I admitted in a whisper, unsure why I was telling him.

"I'm glad you did," he said after a long pause, withdrawing from me. My body ached at the loss. I let my head fall forwards, pressing against the cool wall as I took deep breaths in and out, trying to ground myself. This had been completely unexpected and so fucking good. No, good wasn't the word. Epic. Mind-blowing. Unforgettable.

"I'm glad, too."

A soft kiss was pressed between my shoulder blades, and then the heat of his body was gone. I tilted my head slightly, watching out of the corner of my eye as he tied off the condom and did up his trousers, tucking his shirt back into place. He ran a hand through his hair, ruffling it, and other than its slightly more tousled state, there was no visible evidence of what had just happened, if anyone were to look at him.

Grabbing the pack of wipes that I always kept in my bag, I cleaned away the remaining evidence and tugged my shorts back up. Balling everything up, I pulled back the curtain, crossing over to the bin. When I returned, the man was rubbing his hand over his jaw, and his gaze had shuttered.

As my housemate Ander would say, it looked like he was experiencing post-nut clarity. Unfortunately, he wasn't the only one. Not that I'd regret such an epic fuck, especially not from a man who was one hundred percent my type, but because I'd done this at work. I loved this job. The pay was generous, my boss was incredibly well connected, and my co-workers were great. I should never have done anything to jeopardise it, but here we were.

"I'll make sure no one's around before I send you back out there," I said, and he jerked his head in acknowledgement. I managed to sneak him back through the corridors without anyone catching us, and when we reached the VIP section, he strode off without another word.

We'd never even exchanged names. That wasn't unusual for me, but I had a feeling it was for him.

In the early hours of the morning, when I got home, all thoughts of the hot man were pushed aside when I had to go into crisis mode and deal with my housemate's disaster—being in love with one of our other housemates, Elliot, who happened to be his childhood best friend—and I thought that was the end of it. I thought I'd just carry on as I was, hooking up with hot guys in between work, dance, and uni, living my best gay life.

I thought I'd never see the man who'd dicked me down so perfectly again.

I was wrong.

ONE

JJ

THREE MONTHS LATER

Swinging my gym bag over my shoulder, I jogged down the stairs to be greeted with a loud, aggrieved sigh coming from the kitchen. "This is the worst Tuesday ever. How can this asshole tell me to do another rewrite?"

When I poked my head into the kitchen, I saw Ander seated at the table, his laptop in front of him and his boyfriend, Elliot, by his side, both of them fixated on the screen. They glanced up when I cleared my throat, and Ander gave me a half-hearted attempt at a smile. "Oh. JJ. Hi."

I raised a brow, watching as he took a few deep breaths, composing himself, while Elliot wrapped an arm around his waist and leaned his head on his shoulder.

"You two are so cute," I said, flashing them a grin, and Ander's frustration evaporated.

"We are, aren't we?" He planted a kiss on Elliot's cheek. "You should try it sometime."

"Try what? A relationship? There are way too many dicks in the sea, babe. I'm young, and I'm hot—I can't be selfish. I've got to spread the love."

Ander laughed. "Don't you remember I was the same as you before?"

"No. You were with girls." I pulled a face. I didn't have anything against women—far from it, in fact, not to mention that some of the closest people to me were women—but I was one hundred percent gay. "Anyway, care to tell me what has you so worked up this early on a Tuesday?"

Elliot glanced at Ander. "Ander's not happy because one of our lecturers is making him redo an essay. Dr. Wilder."

"Ahh, the big, bad Dr. Wilder." I'd heard Ander and Elliot complain about their business studies lecturer on more than one occasion. "Sucks to be you, babe."

"Thanks for the sympathy. I have to go and personally deliver it to him at 6:00 p.m. On the dot."

Hmmm. It was about time I saw this infamous uptight asshole for myself. I made a few mental calculations. I had a seminar this morning—after a compulsory coffee stop, followed by a studio session—and then I'd promised to go and visit my grandma. But I could easily make it back by the end of the day...

"You have to personally deliver it?"

Ander huffed. "He said, and I quote, 'I expect a hard copy to be in my hands at 6:00 p.m. sharp, as well as a digital copy submitted through your student portal.'"

"Perfect. I'll deliver it to him."

They both stared at me, Elliot's brows flying up while Ander choked on nothing.

I couldn't stop my laugh from escaping. "You should see your faces." Composing myself, I cleared my throat. "Before you ask why, it's because I'm curious. You've ranted about him enough times, so if anything, it's your fault that I want to see this lecturer who has you so worked up. I have no personal investment because I don't take any of the same courses as you, so it's not as if he can scare me with threats. It'll be fun."

"It won't be fun, but it's a deal. Anything to avoid seeing his face." Ander held up his hand for a high five, but I stepped backwards, blowing him a kiss instead.

"No time for that. Got to go now if I want to fit in a workout this morning. Text me when the essay's ready." I shifted my gym bag on my shoulder. "See you both later." With a wave, I headed out of the house to begin my day.

"You need to find a nice man. I'm not getting any younger, you know, and I need to see you with your one great love before I pass on to higher places." My grandma's eyes sparkled at me over the top of her hand of cards. A violet curl fell over her forehead, and she impatiently brushed it away.

I rolled my eyes. One great love, indeed. "Stop that, G. You're nowhere near ready to kick the bucket. Anyway, I'm responsible now. Don't forget, I'm a parent."

Reaching across the table, she smacked me on the arm. "A snail that you somehow managed to permanently acquire from your friend doesn't count as parenting, Josh."

Shooting her a wounded look, I sighed. "We've been

through this before. It counts. I even have a written joint custody agreement drawn up with Ander. Personally, I think that's very responsible of me."

She beamed at me as she placed a card face up on the table. A three of diamonds. "You're a good boy. You know I only want you to be happy. Now, tell me all your news. Did you choose a piece for your showcase dance?"

Scanning my cards, I thought for a moment and then added my four of clubs to the face-up cards between us. "Not yet. We've narrowed down the group number and started to work on the choreography for the routine, but I'm not sure about my individual dance yet. I need to find my muse."

"These things can't be rushed. Did I tell you about the time I was booked to perform at Elton John's birthday bash, and it took me months to find my muse?"

"Yes. You did. That was the time you ran off with that waiter after your dance and then thought better of it and returned to the party two hours later." My grandma had a penchant for tall tales, skating the line between fiction and reality. She did it for my amusement as well as hers, and we both enjoyed it.

She laughed lightly. "Ah, Mathias. Such a handsome man but so uncouth. Ooh, that reminds me! It almost slipped my mind. George from the second floor is trying to woo me again. Can you believe it? He bought me chocolates. Imported from Switzerland. Be a dear and fetch them for us, would you?"

Laying down my cards, I climbed to my feet, making my way to the sideboard where she kept her treats hidden away.

"Didn't you tell me he was trying to get with Barbara last week?"

"Pfft. That woman is a ho. He saw the light soon enough."

"G! You can't go around saying things like that." Returning with the chocolates, I popped off the lid, reading through the list. Mmm...praline. When I slipped my selected chocolate into my mouth, the rich, creamy flavour burst on my tongue. Delicious.

"I can say whatever I like. It's true." Tapping her fingers on the table, she pointedly cleared her throat. "Don't keep all the chocolates to yourself, Joshua. I taught you better than that."

"So impatient," I tutted, sliding the box across the table. We smiled at each other, and a rush of fondness went through me. My grandma was amazing. She had raised me after my mum had decided that running off with a man she'd just met was more fun than taking responsibility for a baby. My dad had shown up in my teenage years, but after one afternoon with me, during which several revelations led to me being referred to as a raging homosexual, plus a slur that will never be repeated, he'd left me for dust. Grandma, or G, as I called her, was great, though. She'd given me all the parenting I could ever need, in her own slightly chaotically crazy style, and as a result, I'd grown up in a free and accepting home where I could be my authentic self. She was a fucking rock star.

Back in the day, she'd been a performer, singing and dancing in London clubs and cabarets. To hear it from her, she'd brushed shoulders with the rich and famous throughout her working life, and she always had plenty of stories to tell. Granted, most of them were made-up, but I loved her for it. She brought sparkle into my life, and now she was living in this luxury retirement apartment complex with its own packed social calendar and even a cinema, bowling alley, and bar, she probably had even more of a social life than I did.

My grandad had passed away over ten years ago, and although my grandma flirted and even casually "dated" some of the men in the complex, she never wanted anything more. My grandad had been her one great love, as she told it, and she'd never looked at anyone else seriously. She deserved to have fun, though, and I loved that she was thriving here with her friends.

"G, I need your advice." Reaching over the table, I swiped another chocolate from the open box without checking the flavour and then winced as I bit into it, steeling myself for coffee or strawberry creme. Luckily, it was caramel, a flavour I didn't mind.

"You know I'm always available to dole out my pearls of wisdom, my dear. What is it?"

"My showcase dance. Our group dance is most likely going to end up being a combination of ballet and hip-hop moves, but I wanted to incorporate balletic movements into my solo dance. I'm just unsure if it would make me lose points if I were to demonstrate the same technique in both dances."

Her eyes crinkled as she smiled at me. "Dance from the heart. That's all you need to do. Dance from the heart, and the rest will come. When you do that, you shine so brightly, Josh."

A lump came into my throat at the sincerity in her

words. "Okay. Thanks. I...I still don't know exactly what I'm going to do, but I can do that."

"Good." Whipping one of the cards from her hand with a speed that belied her age, she slammed it down on the table. "Ha! An ace of spades. I win."

"Yeah. You win." I grinned at her. "Want another game? Or do you want to tell me about George's attempts to woo you? I've got almost an hour until I need to get back and do a thing for a friend, so—"

"A thing for a friend? Tell me more."

Shaking my head, I began gathering up the playing cards, placing them in a neat pile. "It's nothing important. Ander has to hand in an essay to one of his lecturers, and by all accounts, the guy's an uptight dick, so I said I'd take it to him." Batting my lashes, I smirked at her. "I'm such a good friend."

"A nosy friend, you mean. You want to take a look at this gentleman for yourself, don't you?"

"Well, okay, yes. I am curious. I keep hearing about him, and I know nothing. All my degree teachers love me."

"Of course they do." She stood, a little unsteady for a moment, but waved me off when I rushed around the table to her. "I'm fine, don't fuss. So, this man—you think you're going to charm him?"

"I don't know, but it can't hurt to try. It might make Ander's life easier, at least. If I can smooth the way for him, even a bit, then the guy might stop giving him such a hard time. Do you know he doesn't even let the students refer to him by his first name like all the other teaching staff do? They have to call him 'Sir' or 'Dr. Wilder.'"

Sinking down onto the small sofa in front of the

fireplace, she patted the cushion next to me. "I have no doubt that you'll charm him. Now, come and sit here. We can watch an episode of *The Masked Singer* while I tell you what Lucille told me about Barbara."

With a smile, I did as she said.

TWO

KILLIAN

I pinched my brow and then massaged my temples. This damn headache was getting to me.

It was five fifty, though, so at least my day of work was almost over. Except...it wasn't, was it? My jaw tightened as I remembered that I'd asked Ander Loveridge to hand-deliver his essay to me at 6:00 p.m. What had I been thinking? I should have just asked him to submit it online only, and then I could have left work on time for once. Now, I'd have to sit there and read through his essay before he left because I would not accept another substandard piece of writing. The boy was clever, but I'd noticed that his efforts were minimal when the modules focused on a subject he had little interest in. It was fortunate for him that I looked out for my brightest students, constantly pushing them to do better. It was unfortunate for us both that we'd be stuck in my office when neither of us wanted to be there while I determined if his work was acceptable.

A knock came at the door, and I bit back a growl. I

despised unpunctuality. I'd made sure to state that he was to arrive at six o'clock sharp. Not before, not afterwards.

"Enter," I called, my tone cold, showing my displeasure. The door creaked open, and I had to do a double take.

That wasn't Ander Loveridge standing at my door.

My gaze returned to my screen as I jerked my finger towards the door. "Office hours are over. Come back tomorrow between 3:00 and 4:00 p.m. Close the door on your way out."

There was silence. I glanced back up at the figure, ready to reiterate my words. Then I took a second, longer look.

The young man was dressed simply in an oversized pale blue LSU hoodie, jeans, and white Nikes. A pair of glasses, framed with chunky black rims, were perched on his nose, and his hair was a mop of waves on top of his head. His bright blue eyes were wide, his golden-brown lashes fluttering as he blinked at me, his lips parted in what looked like shock.

A slow chill stole over my body as our gazes connected, and my chest tightened.

He swallowed hard and straightened his shoulders, then took a step forwards, holding something out to me.

"Dr. Wilder."

"It's you," I said hoarsely. "What the fuck is this? What are you doing here?"

He slid the small stack of papers across my desk. "I'm here to deliver Ander's essay."

"Close the door," I commanded, holding his gaze. His nostrils flared, but he didn't argue, simply turning his back to me and softly shutting the door. The air seemed to leave the room with his actions, and I rubbed at my chest, unable to catch a breath.

"Are you okay?"

"Of course I'm fucking not!" My fist slammed down on the desk, making him flinch, and his eyes widened even further. He recovered quickly, though, narrowing his gaze at me.

"I'm not one of your students, so you can drop the attitude, Dr. Wilder."

"What. The fuck. Are you doing here?" I bit out between clenched teeth.

He whipped his glasses off, tugging a case from his pocket and placing them inside, and then came around the desk, stopping right in front of my chair. As I spun to face him, his glare disappeared, and he leaned back against the edge of my desk like he had every right to be in my office, staring down at me with an arched brow.

"Do you have a problem with me being here? Because the last time I saw you, you seemed to enjoy my company. Very much," he purred.

"No." This was not happening.

"No, you don't have a problem?"

"No, I don't want you here. No. This is not happening."

"Okay, okay." He leaned forwards, planting his hands on the arms of my chair. "No need to be like that. I think it's time we were introduced, don't you? I'm JJ. Housemate of Ander and Elliot, two of your students."

What? I stared at him, horrified. "*Housemate?* You're a student here? How old are you? What the fuck were you doing at the club?"

Leaning even closer, his face inches from mine, he

smiled. There was no humour in it. "Yes. Housemate. I am, in fact, a student here, but what I study isn't up for discussion. And to answer your other questions, none of your business, and I work there, okay?"

"It's my fucking business when I've had my cock inside you," I ground out.

His gaze heated, and he shifted forwards, almost in my lap at this point. I stilled underneath him, my dick overriding my consternation, thickening in my trousers. My heart was pounding out of my chest as he leaned even closer. "Mmm. That was an unforgettable night. I don't often do repeats, but I would with you."

A repeat. With a student, who was most likely in his second year if he was living with two of my second-year students. Absolutely not. Never. *Ever.*

"Get. The fuck. Out. *Now.*" Placing my hand on his chest, I launched my chair backwards, the wheels squeaking on the thin carpet tiles, and he lost his balance, collapsing to the floor with a cry. "Out," I repeated, my voice a low growl.

Climbing to his feet, he dusted himself off, shooting me a savage glare. "Bastard. There's no need to resort to violence. You really are as much of an asshole as they say, aren't you?"

"Oh, no. I'm not." Baring my teeth at him in a cold smile, I jabbed my finger towards the door. "I'm worse. Now, fucking get out of my office."

Whirling around, he stormed across the room, yanked the door open, and slammed it hard enough to make the hinges rattle.

Almost as soon as he'd left, remorse hit me.

Shifting my chair back into place, I folded my arms

across the table and dropped my head with a groan. That couldn't have gone any worse. Yes, I'd been blindsided when he entered my office, but I'd handled our entire encounter so badly. He didn't deserve my ire, and I never should have laid a hand on him. There was no excuse for that. And that night in the club, I'd been just as much of an active participant as him, and I hadn't bothered to stop to ask him pertinent questions like, "Are you a student at my university?" I'd been caught up in the moment, and I hadn't wanted to stop.

Fuck.

THREE

JJ

The opening bars of the Seamus Haji remix of Booty Luv's "Boogie 2Nite" blasted through the speakers to the sound of cheers echoing around the club's interior. Niccolò grabbed me around the waist, pulling me into him, his sweat-slicked torso pressing up against mine as he stood up on tiptoes to shout into my ear.

"Has anyone caught your eye yet?"

Good question. My nights at Revolve were the best—hanging out at my favourite gay club in London, dancing with my friends, all of us wearing whatever the fuck we wanted because no one cared or judged us, whatever our body types were. Saying that...more often than not, I ended up in booty shorts, which also happened to be my usual work attire at Sanctuary, but hey—I looked good, so why the fuck not show my body off? No—it wasn't even about that. *Everyone* should wear whatever the fuck they wanted, and who cared what anyone else thought? Your body was your body, and no one else should get a say in what you did with it.

Okay...calm down, JJ. I glanced down at my friend, shaking my head as I tuned back in to the conversation. "Not yet. You?"

He sighed, his glittery pink lips curving into a pout. "Not tonight. I'm on hiatus. I'm filming all day tomorrow."

"Poor baby." I smirked. "It's such a hard life you lead. Your sacrifice will be worth it, though."

"Shay!" Niccolò screeched in my ear, his attention diverted by something to my left. I turned to see our friend strutting towards us like he was still on the runway.

"What's up, bitches?" He grinned at us. "I'm gasping for a drink. The flight from Milan was hellish, I tell you. All that turbulence."

"I suppose I'll have to repeat the words I just said to Nic," I said, pressing a kiss to his cheek and receiving one in return. "It's such a hard life you lead. Here, have mine. I'll get another."

"You're a diamond, darling."

"I know." I blew him another kiss. "Where are Chike and Seth tonight? Weren't they at the show with you?"

"Chike's still in Milan. When I saw him backstage, he was inviting two of the Spanish models back to his hotel room, so I doubt we'll hear from him until tomorrow at the earliest. As for Seth, the poor darling was wiped out after the show. They made him close. He wouldn't stop shaking. But he smashed it, just like we said he would."

"Good." I made my way towards the bar, Niccolò still wrapped around my waist and Shay's fingers clasped between mine. "I'll text him, see how he is."

"He'll appreciate that." Shay clicked his fingers at the bartender. We were regulars, so we were on first-name terms with most of the staff, and this particular bartender, Cole, also happened to be my housemate Elliot's cousin. "Cole! JJ's thirsty!"

Cole gave Shay an exaggerated salute. "One Sex Bomb coming right up."

"Now, tell me, how's my snail?" Drink taken care of, Shay propped a hand on his hip, giving me an expectant look.

"*My* snail, you mean. The snail you left with me when you jetted off to Thailand to dick down every available person in the space of two weeks like the fuckboy you are. If you're nice, I *might* allow you visitation rights. Maybe."

"Snails are so...slimy," Niccolò interjected with a shudder. "I prefer cats."

"Hmmm, is it because they're cute and fluffy with sharp claws, just like you?" I arched a brow at him, and he pretended to growl, raking his pointed, glittering pink nails down my bare chest.

Cole slid the drink across the bar to me, and I tapped my card on the reader. "Thanks, babe." He saluted me, and I lifted my drink in acknowledgement before wrapping my lips around the straw. *Delicious.*

When Cole had disappeared to serve other patrons, the three of us settled back against the bar, scanning the crowds. I was on the lookout for my preferred type—older, dark-haired, taller than me, with broad shoulders and a sharp jawline—but no one had caught my eye yet.

A face flashed through my mind, but I batted the thought away. He'd made it clear that a repeat was off the table, and honestly, it was for the best even if a repeat had been an option, with the fact that he worked at my university, and more importantly, he was Ander and Elliot's lecturer. Things could get messy, and I didn't do messy. I did fun, no strings, both parties aware of what was happening up front.

"JJ. You're not listening to me, are you?" Niccolò tugged on my arm.

Damn Dr. Wilder for invading my thoughts again, just when I'd decided to forget about him. "Sorry, babe. What did you say?"

"I said your friends are here."

"JJ!" A hand waved in my face, and I turned to see Ander and Elliot standing in front of me.

"You made it." I grinned at them both and then took in Ander's shimmery red shorts with a frown. "You raided my wardrobe again, didn't you?"

Ander shrugged. "Hey, I just wanted to join your hot boy clone club." He nodded his head towards Niccolò and Shay. I glanced at them and then looked down at myself. Maybe he had a point since, yes, we were all dressed in some variation of booty shorts. As usual.

"The club's very exclusive, but I suppose we can let you in. Elliot, wanna join, too?"

Elliot bit down on his lip, shaking his head as he unsuccessfully tried to hide an amused smile. "I'll leave that to you, and I'll enjoy the view—" His gaze flicked to Ander's. "—of my boyfriend."

"Good idea." Ander dropped a kiss on the tip of his nose. They really were so cute together. He glanced back at me. "Thanks for doing me that favour earlier, by the way. How did it go?"

Disentangling myself from Niccolò and Shay, I made

my way to the far corner of the bar, followed by my housemates, where there was slightly more breathing room and I could talk to them without raising my voice too much. "It was...fine. He didn't say anything about it."

Ander's brows rose. "That doesn't sound like Dr. Wilder."

That was because I'd lost my head and practically thrown myself at him, and he'd unsurprisingly reacted badly, as blindsided by seeing me as I was him. "No, he seemed a bit distracted." By me.

"Good. That's good. I owe you one."

"Anytime. He's...he's good-looking, isn't he?" I said cautiously. It was dangerous to say too much because both Ander and Elliot were well aware of my preference for older guys.

"JJ. Don't even think about it. That man is an asshole."

"I don't have to like someone to get my dick sucked by them, do I?" I shot back with a smirk, playing it off as a joke.

"You deserve so much better. He's our lecturer, too. That's probably...I don't know if it's against uni policy, but it's...it's—"

"It's Dr. fucking Wilder," Ander finished for Elliot, giving a dramatic shudder. "He's like, everything you're not. Boring and uptight, and he has a major attitude problem, not to mention anger issues. The man seriously needs to get laid and not by you. You're far too good for someone like him."

"This is all hypothetical, right?" Elliot studied me intently, and I hoped that nothing I was thinking was showing on my face.

"Obviously. Look at all the choices I have here. I'm never short of options, you know that."

They both visibly relaxed, and I bit back uncharacteristic words that wanted to fly from my mouth. Words of defence. It was ridiculous. I didn't know anything about Dr. Wilder other than the fact he was an extremely good fuck and extremely moody when he was caught off guard. I didn't even know his first name. And what I *did* know was that a repeat was very much off the table.

It was time for a change of subject. "Come on. It's Throwback Tuesday. Let's get you both a drink, and then we can hit up the dance floor and make the most of this retro music."

The subject of Dr. Wilder was instantly dropped, forgotten as Ander struck a pose, fist pumping the air. But by the end of the night, after I'd uncharacteristically turned down the fifth person who had propositioned me, I was beginning to worry that he wasn't so forgettable after all.

FOUR

KILLIAN

"Working late again? You do realise that everyone else has left the building, don't you?"

I glanced up from my computer to see Gage peering around my door, frowning.

"You're still here," I pointed out.

"Only because I had that meeting with the vice chancellor. Stuart left hours ago." He leaned against the door frame, folding his arms across his chest. "It's time to leave. We can grab a drink on the way to the Tube if you want."

The "if you want" was heavily emphasised. I knew he wouldn't leave me alone unless I agreed. To be fair to him, he left me in peace most of the time...until his conscience prodded him to do something, and then he made it his personal mission to get me to socialise. He couldn't seem to understand that I didn't fucking *like* socialising. I hated making awkward small talk. It was pointless, in my opinion.

With a heavy sigh, I exited out of the university portal,

beginning the process of shutting my computer down. "One drink. Then I need to get back. These essays aren't going to mark themselves."

Gage rolled his eyes. "Yeah, yeah. I know." As I picked up my briefcase and flipped the switch on my desk lamp to turn it off, he shook his head. "I know you're the principal lecturer, but you don't have that much more work than me. You need a better work-life balance. And you don't even have the excuse of being married to be boring like Stuart."

My jaw clenched. We'd gone round and round with this discussion so many times. "Stuart being married doesn't mean he's boring. It means he wants to spend time with his wife. And I do plenty of things in my free time."

"Course you do," he muttered, stepping aside to let me exit my office. "Sitting alone in your flat doesn't count. I'm single, and you don't see me staring at the same four walls for hours on end."

"Gage." The warning in my tone was implicit, and he immediately relented.

"Sorry. I'll say no more. Let's have this drink, and I'll consider my social duty done."

"Until the next time you pester me about it."

"Until then," he agreed, shooting me a grin. "Speaking of the next time, are you planning to bring anyone to the spring faculty dinner?"

"I'm not planning to bring anyone because I'm not planning to go." My voice echoed in the empty stairwell as we made our way down to the ground floor. "It isn't compulsory."

"Ah, but that's where you're wrong. If you want to go from principal lecturer to professor and department head—

which I know is in your two-year plan, so don't even bother denying it—you have to put in the work. And I'm not talking about the academic work. You need to show that you're worthy of the position. It's never too early to make an effort."

"Two-year plan," I muttered.

"Kill. Your plans have plans. Your life is structured like a..." He cast around for words, settling on, "A straitjacket."

"Sorry, did you want a drink, or did you want to list my faults? Shall we make a *plan* to do that another time?"

"It's not a bad thing." His hand lifted as if he was going to pat my shoulder, but at my narrowed eyes, he thought better of it, dropping his arm with a sigh. "Mate, listen to me. You're, like, an academic genius. You're the youngest principal lecturer LSU has ever had in our faculty. You've put in the work, and it's taken you places. All I'm saying is if you want to further your career, which I know you do, you have to start putting in a different kind of work."

"I don't want to talk about it." As we strode across the campus, I clenched and unclenched my fists, my hands hidden in the pockets of my light wool coat. Gage was right, of course. My dream was to earn a professorship and the position of head of the LSU business school in the next two years, and yes, I was well aware that it would involve a level of socialisation I was uncomfortable with. I was still weighing up the pros and cons. It was ridiculous, but I had neither the patience nor the ability for successful small talk, let alone schmoozing with the people who made the big decisions.

"Consider the subject dropped. Let's move on to a more

important discussion—what are we going to drink? I hear The George has a new seasonal IPA on tap."

"Probably that," I murmured, distracted for a moment as my attention caught on a flash of wavy brown hair and long legs disappearing around a corner.

My heart thudded in my chest.

No. I couldn't think about *him*. I refused to think about him. Of course, it was likely that I'd spot him on or around campus, but I hoped it would only ever be at a distance.

My thoughts drifted in the one direction I hadn't wanted them to go. Again. Neither Gage nor Stuart had recognised him at the club, so it was unlikely he was studying one of the business or technology subjects. With over two hundred and thirty courses on offer at the university, though, that barely narrowed it down.

I hated this urge to discover more. He'd been appearing in my thoughts with increased frequency ever since he'd come into my office, and enough was enough.

Squaring my shoulders, I firmly pushed JJ out of my mind. Suddenly, a drink sounded like a great idea.

I turned to Gage. "Forget the ale. I'm in the mood for shots."

His brows flew up as he stared at me. "Who are you, and what have you done with Dr. Wilder?"

"Maybe I decided you're right. I do need a better work-life balance." It had nothing to do with the need to rid my mind of blue eyes, soft lips, and a perfectly sculpted body... Fuck. The sooner he left my mind, the better.

"You definitely do, but possibly not on a school night." As Gage pushed open the door to the pub, we were hit by a wall of noise, immediately surrounded by people who seemed as if they were having the time of their lives. He took a look around us, nodded once, and then grabbed my arm, dragging me into the fray. "On second thoughts, you need to loosen up, and who knows when you'll be in this kind of mood again. Let's do it."

FIVE

KILLIAN

This was a part of campus I'd never ventured onto before and never had any reason to. Before now.

Sipping from my takeaway coffee cup, the bitter liquid burning my throat as I swallowed, I stepped inside the performing arts building.

What was I doing here? If anyone saw me... The likelihood of any of these students recognising me was hopefully minimal, but there was still a chance, and there would be faculty members who would certainly know who I was. It still didn't deter me, though, my footsteps echoing across the tiled floor as I made my way through the building, bypassing the theatre, and followed the signs to the dance studios.

Joshua James Everett. Studying for a Bachelor of Arts in dance. Twenty years old.

I knew those facts, thanks to my slightly unethical use of the student records system a few nights ago, home alone and not thinking straight after one too many ill-advised shots with Gage at The George. Now that I had his name, I also had his email address, which was publicly available to both students and faculty members if one knew the name of the student or staff member. I'd also used my staff privileges to obtain a copy of the current timetable for second-year students studying his degree, and while I couldn't quite believe I'd gone so far in my drunken state, I was yet to feel any real form of regret—other than the regret that accompanied a painful hangover. That in itself was worrying. I did, however, feel shock at myself that I'd let myself get to the point of employing stalking tactics with a student who was *ten years younger* than I was.

It was irresponsible. It was a blatant abuse of power. It was wrong.

But still, I continued forwards.

When I reached dance studio 2, I stopped, composing myself, and then glanced through the large windows that opened into the hallway.

I saw him straight away. My breath caught in my throat, and my traitorous cock stirred in my trousers at the sight of him. He was alone, sensually curving his body backwards in front of the long wall of mirrors. Dressed simply in a pair of black dance tights, with his feet bare and his beautiful, sculpted torso exposed, his hair damp and skin glistening with exertion, he took my breath away. I'd never had such a visceral reaction to anyone before, man or woman, and yet this student that was far too young and wrong for me had completely stolen my attention from the moment I'd first laid eyes on him. But regardless, I shouldn't be here. He was pure sunshine, and I was jaded, angry, uptight... All those things that people said behind my back and to my face were true. Even if those facts weren't true, he was still out of my reach, both with his age and his status as a student here. I couldn't allow myself to get close to him. I couldn't allow myself to dull his sparkle.

No, instead, I'd stand outside the studio and watch him from afar like the stalker I was turning out to be.

"Excuse me! Are you here for JJ? I mean, hi, can I help you with anything?"

My head shot around to see a petite blonde eyeing me with interest, her hands on her hips.

"No. I'm just..." Caught off guard, I held up my coffee cup as if it would substitute for words I didn't have.

"Aww, you brought him coffee! That's so sweet! He'll appreciate that, what with his caffeine addiction." Before I knew what was happening, slim fingers had wrapped around my wrist, and I was being pulled towards the door to the dance studio. Still in shock, I allowed myself to go, my brain frozen and unable to process what was happening.

"JJ!" the girl boomed in a voice far too loud for such a petite person.

"Alyssa! There's no need to shout." JJ's lips curved up, but his smile was instantly wiped away when he spotted me standing next to her. His mouth dropped open in shock, a furrow appearing between his brows. Fuck. This was terrible.

"He brought you coffee." The girl dropped her grip on my wrist, bounding over to JJ and throwing her arms around him. "Isn't that sweet?"

His gaze darted back to mine as he returned her hug. "Sweet," he repeated slowly, a question in his eyes. "Hey, Aly, can you find Leo? I think he's in studio 4. We need to work on our group choreo."

She nodded, releasing him, and danced away, the door closing behind her.

When she was gone, JJ prowled towards me, and I remained frozen in place. My mouth was dry, and my heart was hammering. I was used to order in my life, and now, nothing was going to plan.

"Dr. Wilder. What a surprise. I hear you brought me coffee." He lifted the cup from my unresisting grip, took a sip, and then pulled a face. "Ugh. What is that?"

"Americano. No milk."

"Next time, bring me something sweeter, please. Preferably with syrup." His humour dying away, he studied me from beneath his lashes. "I know you didn't come to bring me coffee. The last time we spoke, I kind of got the impression that you'd rather not run into me again. What are you really doing here?"

I shook my head, at a loss. I had no explanation, so I told him the truth. "I don't know, Joshua. At a minimum, I should apologise for my behaviour in my office."

Surprise flashed in his gaze. "Joshua. No one calls me that, apart from G. And even then, it doesn't happen often. Usually when I've misbehaved. I accept your apology, by the way."

A weight I hadn't known I was holding lifted. "G?" Raising a brow, I held out my hand. "I suppose I should introduce myself. Dr. Killian Wilder."

That gorgeous smile curved over his lips, thawing an infinitesimal portion of the permafrost around my heart. "G is my grandma. Nice to officially meet you, Killian. It's a surprise and very much a pleasure. How did you find me?"

"Anyone can see the timetables if they log in to the portal."

"They can if they know the course I'm doing, which I don't remember telling you."

I closed the distance between us, lowering my head. The urge to kiss those plump, pink lips was so strong that I could barely restrain myself from taking what I wanted until I was sated and this madness left me. Somehow, I resisted. "I have my ways."

"You know, I don't think I've ever had a stalker before." He placed a hand on my chest, sliding it up to the hollow of my throat, making my heart rate increase beneath his touch. "Especially not one as delicious as you."

"Delicious?"

"Mmm. Very." The low, sultry tone of his voice had my cock responding almost instantly. Rising onto the balls of his feet, he leaned right in, his lips almost brushing mine. "Are you here to tell me you've changed your mind? You want a repeat of the night in the club? Because I'd be verrry interested if so."

At his words, something ignited between us. A hot spark, setting my nerve endings alight.

All my objections went out of the window.

"Yes," I growled, my self-control fraying and snapping as I closed the distance between us, our lips connecting. He tasted just as sweet as I remembered but with a hint of the bitterness of my coffee. Fuck. I couldn't get enough. I wanted to deepen the kiss, to stroke my tongue against his, to taste, and taste, and taste.

"Not here." Tearing his mouth away from mine after only a second or two, he stared around us, wild-eyed. "Fuck.

What was I thinking? What am I doing? This is the second time I've lost my mind around you. Alyssa and Leo will be here any second. *Fuck.* Look what you did." I followed his gaze downwards to see the outline of a gorgeous but rather prominent erection, and with the dance tights he was wearing, there was no chance of hiding it. My own rapidly hardening erection was almost as obvious, but thankfully, I was wearing a light wool overcoat, buttoned up, that easily hid the evidence.

He tipped his head back with a groan, raking a hand through his hair.

"Fucking gorgeous," I murmured, my cock throbbing as I took in his arousal. I hadn't become aroused this quickly in a long time. Not since the club, and before that...it had been even longer. *Much* longer. Not only that, but I couldn't remember ever being so sexually attracted to someone in my life. This wasn't me. I didn't do things like this, ever.

He glanced back up at me, heat in his gaze. "There's the man I remember from the club. Not...whoever that was in the office. You're—"

Cutting himself off, his mouth snapped shut as the door opened and his friends entered the studio. When he dropped into a crouch, I moved swiftly towards them, directing their attention towards me to allow him time to compose himself. Something inside me knew exactly what to do. It was a natural instinct to protect him. To make sure his vulnerabilities weren't exposed.

"Alyssa, and...Leo, was it? I'm Killian. It's a pleasure to meet you both. You're Josh—JJ's colleagues?"

Leo shifted from foot to foot, staring down at the floor, but Alyssa beamed at me. "Yep! We're JJ's dance partners for the showcase. We're doing a group dance together. Want to watch us practise?"

"If that would be acceptable. Where should I stand?" As long as their attention remained on me while JJ was composing himself, everything would be okay.

Leo finally lifted his gaze from the floor, eyeing me warily. "Y-you're...you're..." he began, his cheeks flushing. "Never mind," he whispered, spinning away and running towards the corner of the room where an iPad was set on a dock on the floor.

"Don't worry about him. He's super shy. Performing in front of people is hard for him. Having you here will be a good test, actually." Alyssa gave me another bright smile. "Sit or stand anywhere. The back wall is good. You can see us from the back and the front that way because you'll be facing the mirror. We'll go through a few warm-up stretches —or I will since the others have already been dancing, and then we'll do a run-through of the routine so far before we start breaking it down."

Music began playing from the wall-mounted speakers, and Leo straightened up, glancing over at us, his cheeks still flushed, before his gaze darted away again. I studied him. Something about him looked familiar, which meant that it was highly likely that he'd either been in one of my classes or had classes in the same building I taught in. Neither option was good, but there was nothing I could do now he'd seen me.

As Alyssa began her warm-up, I quickly strode to the back of the room to create as much distance between myself and JJ as possible. When I had a solid surface behind me, I fixed my gaze back on JJ. He went through the same warm-up moves as Alyssa, and then Leo joined them after some coaxing from JJ, the three of them stretching and contorting their bodies.

There were three, but I only had eyes for one person.

Taking a sip of my coffee, I asked myself what I was doing here in this dance studio. I still didn't have an answer, and now I couldn't leave.

Alyssa skipped over to the iPad, and the music stopped. She glanced over at JJ, who nodded, taking a stance that looked balletic—ramrod-straight posture, legs together, with one foot turned out. Alyssa took her place next to him, with Leo on the other side, and the three of them held themselves still for a long moment.

Then, the music began. JJ curved his body forwards. After a moment's hesitation from Leo, followed by a pointed look from Alyssa, they began moving in sync towards JJ, twisting to the side and stretching out their arms. As their bodies curled over, JJ straightened up and kept going, bending backwards, so smooth and graceful that I couldn't stop looking at him even if I'd tried. He swung up onto his toes, pirouetting and then pulling Alyssa into a spin, then placing her back down, not pausing for a beat before he reached for Leo, gripping his waist and lifting him into the air.

The bass kicked in as soon as Leo touched back down, and the three of them moved together seamlessly in a coordinated sequence of movements that looked like something from a music video. Not that I'd watched many music videos, but I knew enough to appreciate that the three of them were very, very good.

And JJ—he was the star. Undeniably.

As they danced, I lost myself in the story they were telling with their bodies, the music filtering through every corner of the room, filling my senses with this audio and visual spectacle that I was getting to see in its raw form. Raw, but already so fluid and so beautiful.

The music came to an end, and I scrubbed my hand over my face, trying to catch my breath. What was this man doing to me? I didn't think poetic thoughts. I didn't watch dance performances. And I certainly didn't stalk students on the campus where I worked.

JJ pulled the other two dancers to him, gesturing with his hands as he conferred with them. When they stepped back, he jogged over to me. "Okay. Leo's...struggling a bit. I know we're just practising, and you're only one person, but he hasn't performed in front of anyone outside of our dance group..."

I took the out, unsure if it was because I wanted and needed to leave or if he wanted me to. "I understand. I'll go." Pausing, I took a minute to take him in, his heaving chest, his sparkling eyes, his soft smile. He was so beautiful and so very wrong for me. "You were amazing. But this was a mistake. I should never have come here."

He bit down on his lip, nodding, accepting my words, and even though it shouldn't have hurt, it did. "Yeah. It's probably for the best. I'll see you around, Killian."

My name on his lips sounded so sweet. I swallowed. "Goodbye, Joshua."

With a nod to the other two dancers, I walked out the door.

SIX

KILLIAN

"One Americano and one—" Pausing for a moment, I scanned the wall menu to make sure I had the correct order. "One caramel Frappuccino with whipped cream."

The barista nodded, thrusting the card reader at me and taking my name. When I went to the other end of the counter to await my prepared order, I blew out a heavy breath. What was I doing?

During the detour to the performing arts block, I berated myself, but I kept walking until I was right outside. Thankfully, I'd timed it just right, and I saw a flash of blonde hair entering the building ahead of me.

"Alyssa," I called out, and she stopped dead in her tracks, spinning around to face me. When she recognised me, she gave me a small smile.

"Back again?"

Shaking my head, I held out the Frappuccino. "Not today, but I would appreciate it if you could deliver this to JJ."

Her smile widened, and she shot me a cheeky wink. "Two days in a row. I knew you were keen on him."

It took every ounce of my self-control to refrain from a cutting remark and to allow her to take the coffee when all I wanted to do was to take it and leave. I shouldn't be here. What on earth had possessed me to buy JJ coffee, let alone stand in the shop for a good ten minutes, deliberating which one he'd prefer?

The second the coffee cup was in her hand, I spun on my heel and stalked away in the direction of the building I was supposed to be heading to all along. Angry and frustrated and confused by my own actions, my jaw set, I threw open the door to the lecture hall with a loud bang, throwing my briefcase down at the foot of the lectern. The students inside exchanged wide-eyed glances, scurrying to their seats as quickly as they could, unpacking laptops and notebooks from bags, making far too much fucking noise.

"Take your seats and quieten down. This is not social hour. You will sit in silence, and you will pay attention. Your only tasks for the next hour are to listen and take notes on the subject matter. Do I make myself clear?" Silence reigned, and I gritted my teeth, slamming my palm down on the lectern and raising my voice. "Do I make myself clear?"

A chorus of tentative "yeses" sounded, and with that, the lecture began.

An hour later, my voice was hoarse from berating incompetent students, and my mood had plummeted even lower. I dismissed the students, shovelled everything into my briefcase, and then headed for my office to regroup before the next lecture began. Inside, I locked the door and slumped at my desk, rubbing at my brow. Another headache was brewing, and I did not need this on top of everything else.

I flipped the switch to turn on my monitor and wiggled the mouse to wake the computer. There were still forty-five minutes until the next lecture, and I had emails to deal with from yet more incompetent students, as well as coursework to mark. I knew I'd end up working through lunch as usual, but it was a small price to pay to allow me a little bit of downtime in the evenings, and it kept me from having to make pointless small talk with other faculty members in the staff canteen. A takeaway sandwich or soup did the job, and most importantly, it was quick.

What felt like five minutes later, my phone alarm sounded, reminding me I needed to get ready for my next lecture. With a sigh, I stretched my body, stiff from sitting hunched over in my chair, and checked my laptop to make sure the slideshow I'd prepared was ready to go. My mood was as low as it had been earlier, but I vowed to keep a lid on it. The students didn't deserve my ire—well, some did, but not all, especially not when that ire should have been directed at myself.

What the fuck had I been thinking?

JJ

"What's on your mind?"

I motioned to my ear, and Ander leaned closer, shouting to be heard over the volume of the music. It was lucky that the Mansions, the row we lived on, was made up of student houses. A street of large Victorian double-fronted residences, they were more or less identical in layout. Tonight, the residents of number 3 were throwing a party for their neighbour Tina's birthday—one of the housemates of number 5—and I was several drinks in already. Truth be told, I wasn't a big drinker, but after the confusing interaction I'd had this morning, I needed it. Just enough that I could relax, not enough that I'd have a hangover tomorrow. I couldn't afford to get wasted, not when I had so much on my plate. Between my dance degree, work, volunteering, my packed social life, and the time I spent with my grandma, there wasn't time for anything that would keep me out of action.

"I said, what's on your mind?" he repeated, and I raised a shoulder in a lazy shrug.

"Nothing in particular. Man trouble." I glanced over at Elliot, who was playing poker with several of our housemates and people from number 3 and 5, his bottom lip pulled between his teeth as he contemplated his hand of cards. "Not that you have to worry about such things anymore."

He smirked at me. "I never had to worry about *man* trouble, but girl trouble, yeah. What's the matter? Someone being clingy? Won't take no for an answer?"

"Mmm, not exactly." Was it clingy if Ander's standoffish, supposedly uptight lecturer showed up at my dance rehearsal? Clingy wasn't the right word for it. "He's... confusing."

Ander threw his arm across my shoulders, gesturing at the crowds. "No need for confusion when you have all these options. You're a great kisser—I should know. Go and treat someone to your expertise."

"Aww, babe. It sounds like you're angling for a repeat of our kiss." I laughed when he pulled a face at me. "I'm joking. That was...a bizarre experience."

"You can say that again. At least it helped me to realise that Elliot was the one I enjoyed kissing."

"Yeah. You're welcome for that." My distracted gaze landed on a guy standing in the corner of the room, arms folded across his chest. "You invited Finn?"

Ander followed my gaze, his brows pulling together. "I didn't invite him specifically, but the whole football team was invited. You can't expect him to stay away."

I jabbed a manicured finger into his chest. "Just keep him away from me. Far away."

"You need to stop holding a grudge." With an eye roll,

Ander dropped his arm from my shoulders. "He threw up on you during freshers' week, JJ. That was, like, eighteen months ago!"

"He ruined my shoes. They were a limited-edition Nike and Gucci collab. They were irreplaceable!"

"Oh, bloody hell, you're not still complaining about those shoes, are you?" Another of our neighbours, Liam, came strolling over, his arm slung around his boyfriend's waist.

"You can fuck off," I told him in the politest way possible. Speaking of grudges, I could swear the guy still held a grudge against me for daring to flirt with his boyfriend before they were even officially together. When I gave him a sweet smile, he glared at me. Yep, he definitely still held a grudge.

His boyfriend elbowed him in the side, and his glare instantly melted away, replaced with a sheepish look. "Sorry, JJ." When his boyfriend kissed his cheek, he flushed, a smile curving over his lips, and it made me smile, too. Fuck the bastard for being so cute that I'd forgive him for acting like an asshole.

A sudden thought struck me, and I gasped out loud, clasping my hands to my chest. "Fucking hell! I'm the fairy godmother, aren't I?"

Three sets of eyes swung to me, the expressions ranging from amusement to confusion.

"You two." I pointed between Liam and his boyfriend, Noah. "If it hadn't been for me flirting with Noah, you'd never have got your shit together."

"Bit of a stretch," Liam muttered, but I was still talking, my attention going to Ander.

"You. Where do I begin? The kiss. Revolve. Sid. A shoulder to lean on."

"Yeah, yeah, you're our fairy godmother and my joint snail dad." Ander pressed a loud, exaggerated kiss to my cheek. "When does the fairy godmother get his own prince?"

I drew myself up to my full height. "This fairy godmother doesn't need a prince. There are too many frogs —aka hot boys—to kiss. See you all later." With that parting shot, I whirled around dramatically and stalked off. I had no destination in mind, but the conversation had reminded me of one thing. There were plenty of hot guys out there, and tonight, I was going to make the most of it.

An hour later, I was teetering in the space between tipsy and drunk, so I'd switched to water. I'd made a circuit of the house, but no one had caught my eye. This was a dire situation.

Making a snap decision, I opened *HookdLDN*, the local hook-up app, scrolling to see who was nearby. Ooh... someone was in my vicinity. A new person. Tapping on their profile, I scrolled through the pictures they'd added. Mmm, yeah, they'd do. No headshots, but as long as they were reasonably good at sucking dick, I'd take it.

Instead of going into my messages, I took a closer look at the photos, noting their build and the defining features on show—hands, tattooed arms, thick thighs... Then, I placed my phone back in my pocket and aimed for the centre of the lounge, taking a good look at every guy I passed. This was going to be a treasure hunt.

I hit the jackpot when I reached the first-floor landing. Discreetly checking my phone, I compared the photos with the guy slouching against the wall, a joint hanging from his lips. His short-sleeved T-shirt meant his tattoos were on show, and yep, they matched the pictures. He wasn't my usual type, but he was pretty hot and, according to his profile, into sucking cock.

Perfect.

Coming to a stop in front of him, I plucked the joint from his lips and put it out against the wall, ignoring his shout of protest. "You won't be needing that anymore."

"What the fuck?"

Angling my head to his ear, I leaned in, tucking the remains of his joint into his pocket. "I can think of something better to put in your mouth."

His breath hitched, and I smiled. That was all the confirmation I needed. Sliding my fingers between his, I tugged him away from the wall, heading in the direction of the bathroom. When we reached our destination, I cut in at the front of the queue and shoved him inside, ignoring the aggrieved noises coming from the hallway as I clicked the lock into place. "Sorry for the inconvenience," I called through the wood. "It's a bit of an emergency."

When I turned back to face the guy, he blinked at me. "Bit forward, aren't you?"

I shrugged. "I know what I want, and I don't see any point in dancing around it. Let's not waste any more time."

"Okay. I can agree with you there." Lowering himself to his knees, he rested his hands on my thighs, his face deliciously close to my semi-hard cock. "Are you gonna return the favour when I'm done?"

"If you're good, I might think about it."

The words came out on autopilot in my usual flirty tone,

but what he'd said... What was it that made my cock decide to deflate rather than perk up further? I had a reasonably attractive man on his knees in front of me, and I definitely wasn't opposed to giving a blowjob. Loved it, in fact.

"Are you sure you really want to do this?" He raised his brows, eyeing my crotch. "It seems like your words are speaking louder than your actions."

"Fuck." I threaded my fingers through his hair, willing my dick to cooperate as I angled my hips forwards. A face appeared in my mind, but I pushed it away. I drew the line at thinking about a different person when someone was getting me off. "Too much alcohol."

With a smirk, he unbuttoned my snug-fitting jeans. "When I get my mouth on you, that won't be a problem."

Tightening my grip on his hair, I leaned back against the bathroom wall, tuning out the pounding of someone's fist on the other side. This was what I needed. A hot, willing mouth. Normality. Something that would make me forget a certain, very much off-limits man who was haunting my thoughts.

"Dude. How much have you had to drink? I don't think this is gonna happen."

I blinked down at the guy, realising what he'd already noticed—that my cock had gone from half-mast to completely fucking soft. This was completely unprecedented. What the fuck was happening to me?

"Sorry." I batted his hands away, quickly buttoning my jeans. My cheeks were hot, and my heart was racing. "The drinks must've been stronger than I thought."

"You don't say." He rolled his eyes as he followed me out of the door, muttering under his breath, his uncomplimentary words accompanied by angry noises from the people waiting in the queue. I ignored them all, pushing through the crowds, not stopping until I'd exited the house, entered number 1, and made my way up the stairs to the top floor. When I reached my room, I threw myself down on my bed with a groan.

Fuck Dr. Killian fucking Wilder, the sexy, cockblocking bastard.

I needed to forget him.

No. First, I needed to find out why he'd brought me coffee. Why he'd stalked my dance studio. Why he'd stayed.

Then, I could forget him and move on with my life.

EIGHT

KILLIAN

S taring at my computer screen, with an uneaten sandwich wrapped in foil next to me, I rubbed at my tired eyes. The words were swimming in front of my eyes, a sure sign that I needed sleep. Taking a sip of my now-cold coffee, I grimaced. Washing the taste away with bottled water and a mint from my desk drawer, I got up, walking over to the window and staring down at the campus beneath me. From up here, watching the people below in their groups, meandering along or moving with intent, all having places to go and people to see, I wondered how it was possible that I'd reached the age of thirty and never developed any truly close relationships. Even as a student, I'd found it difficult, never experienced that bond that so many others said they developed with their peers at such a crucial time of their lives. No doubt a counsellor would tell me it was all to do with the fact that I'd spent my childhood bouncing around foster homes, never forming connections. There was never any point when I knew I'd always move on.

It was better this way. I was used to my own company.

A soft knock interrupted my thoughts, and I steeled myself. "Come in."

Light footsteps followed the quiet creak of the door opening and closing. Gripping the windowsill, I remained where I was, unseeing.

"The coffee. What was that all about?"

I exhaled heavily. Some part of me had known it would be him. I had no answer to give. I couldn't even explain it to myself.

"Killian." JJ's voice sounded right behind me. A hand slid onto my arm. "Look at me."

Against my better judgement, I turned around, too tired to gather my defences.

He stared at me for a long moment, his gaze searching, and then he did something I wasn't expecting. He reached up, cupping the back of my neck as his other arm wound around my shoulders, and pulled me into him. My body stiffened, my fists clenching at my sides.

"You look like you could use a hug," he murmured against my ear. "Let yourself have this."

At his words, I breathed out, tentatively lifting my arms to loosely wrap around his back. My hands were shaking.

"That's it." His fingers massaged the back of my neck, and I relaxed even further, breathing out against him, my arms pulling him closer to me without any conscious thought.

When was the last time someone had hugged me like this? For no reason other than to provide comfort? I couldn't even remember. And yet here was this boy with the sunshine smiles, giving me what I didn't even know I needed.

There was a lump in my throat that wouldn't go away.

When he released me, he directed me to sit down. "We're going to talk about what you bringing me coffee means, but not yet. Right now, you're going to sit down while I—" His gaze caught on something on my desk, his brows pulling together and his mouth turning down. "Have you eaten today?"

I followed his gaze to my uneaten sandwich. "I worked through lunch, and I must've forgotten."

He leaned over, prodding at the sandwich with distaste, shaking his head. "The bread's gone hard now. You can't eat this. It's probably been sitting here for hours, hasn't it?"

I didn't reply, but I didn't need to. With an angry huff of breath, JJ wrapped the sandwich back up, throwing it into the wastepaper basket. Then, he headed over to the door, crouching down, and I heard the distinctive sound of a zipper opening, followed by a rustling noise. When he appeared again, he placed two items down in front of me. "This is all I have in my bag, but it's better than a stale sandwich. Protein bar and an apple. Eat them."

I almost smiled at his bossy tone as I reached for the protein bar, tearing into the wrapper. He was the one to smile then, and he returned to me, hopping up onto the edge of my desk next to my chair. Had it been anyone else, I wouldn't have allowed it, but I seemed to break my rules for him all too easily.

"I know we don't know each other, but if there's anything you want to get off your chest, I'm a good listener."

It was easier to focus on the protein bar, to shake my

head as I filled my mouth so I didn't have to respond to his comment. JJ didn't speak again, and when I risked a glance up at him, he was staring down at his hands.

"It's been a long day," I said.

JJ nodded. "Any reason?"

Finishing up the last of the protein bar, I reached for the apple. "I'm tired, and I worked through lunch instead of taking a break."

"Okay. There's probably no point in me telling you that you need to take regular breaks and get some sleep, is there?" He shot me a wry smile as I took a bite of the crisp, juicy fruit.

Shaking my head, I climbed to my feet and carefully placed the apple down on the desk. I pushed my chair back and then came to stand in front of him.

His eyes widened when I lifted my hand, placing my knuckles beneath the smooth skin of his chin, and tilted his head up. "Killian."

"Thank you," I said simply, lowering my head and brushing my mouth over his soft lips.

The kiss was fleeting, and it was ill-advised, yet it wasn't enough. When I lifted my head again, I lowered my hand, taking a purposeful step back to create some distance between us.

"No." JJ glared at me.

"No?" My heart felt as if it had been jump-started from our one brief kiss, new energy thrumming through my body. "No, what?"

"No," he said again. "You don't bring me fucking coffee, get me worried about you, and then tease me with that excuse for a kiss."

"What would you prefer I did, Joshua? Don't bring you coffee? Refuse to allow you into my office? Stay away from your tempting fucking mouth?" I found myself leaning closer again, my hands planted on the desk on either side of him. Our faces were mere inches apart.

"No," he bit out. "I want you to stop teasing me and take what we both want."

"What we shouldn't want."

"I'm finding it hard to care about what we should and shouldn't want when all the blood from my brain is currently in my dick."

There was a moment when we paused, breathing hard, our gazes locked on one another, and then the spark between us ignited, setting us alight.

We lunged for each other. My mouth came down on his, hard, one of my hands going to his hip to yank him into me. He widened his legs, right on the edge of my desk, and I pressed forwards, my erection sliding against his. Moaning against my lips, he wrapped his legs around me, his hands clutching at my shoulders to hold him in place as he opened his mouth for me.

"What are you doing to me?" he panted, arching his body, his hips thrusting forwards, desperate for friction.

"What are you doing to me?" I had no explanation for what was happening between us. Sweeping my arms beneath his thighs, I lifted him, staggering over to the door. Pressing him up against the solid surface, I fumbled for the lock, clicking it into place before I attacked his mouth with a vengeance. I poured every ounce of stress, frustration, and anger into my kiss, and he returned it with enthusiasm, writhing against me, hot and hard and so fucking beautiful in my arms.

When he tilted his head back, my mouth went to his throat, biting and kissing the column of his neck.

"No...marks. Can't. Dance. Work." His voice had taken on a rasp, and my cock grew impossibly harder at the knowledge that I'd been the one to affect him this way. "I had enough questions after...after you'd left that...that chain of bruises around my neck after the club."

"Fuck." I kissed back up his neck, over his jaw, capturing his lips again. "Can't get enough of kissing you."

"Killian. I want—" He untangled his legs from my waist, standing upright and pushing me back. "Will you let me?"

I was incapable of denying either of us. Whatever he wanted, he could have. Giving him a short nod, I watched as he lowered himself to his knees.

He looked up at me, his pupils blown and his plush lips shining from our kisses. Leaning forwards, he slid his face up the side of my erection, making my cock throb, precum already soaking through my boxer briefs. "I want to suck your cock."

My hand slid into his silky hair, lightly tugging him forwards, increasing the pressure. "*Fuck.* Do it."

He mouthed at the tip of my cock through my trousers, his fingers making quick work of undoing my belt, and I groaned. Dimly, I registered we were in my office, and there was a possibility of both staff and students coming by, but I'd locked the door, and now I had him on his knees, there was nothing that would make me stop this from happening short of JJ changing his mind.

When my trousers were open, he lifted his head, his

finger tracing over the outline of my erection and then circling the tip.

"I've dreamed about this big cock," he said with an absolutely sinful smile on his face. "Dreamed of sucking it, of riding it, of you holding me down and pounding in and out of me. I've—"

"Fuck," I ground out, the cock in question throbbing and leaking, his rasped words and teasing touch sending me so close to the edge. My grip tightened in his hair, tugging his head towards me. "Need to fill your mouth. Take me out, now."

He moaned, finally freeing my hard length, his tongue gliding over his lips as he gripped the base. His pupils were so wide as he stared at my erection. "So fucking hot."

Lowering his head, he took me into his mouth, all the way down to where his hand was gripping me. It was fucking perfection. It had been so long since I'd had anyone's lips around me, and it was ridiculous how close to the edge I already was. Then, his talented tongue got to work, sliding over my erection, tonguing at the sensitive spot beneath the head. Using his lips and tongue to expose the tip of my cock, he stroked across the slit, licking up my precum while his hand worked the rest of my shaft. When he took me deeper again, his fingers circled my balls, gently tugging them, and I groaned.

"Fuck. I'm going to come down your throat." I'd barely managed to get the sentence out when my cock pulsed and jerked. He swallowed my cum down with enthusiasm, moaning around my cock, drawing out my orgasm. My legs were suddenly weak, and I staggered to the wall and collapsed against the solid surface, breathing hard.

JJ stared up at me, his tongue darting out to lick up a drop of my cum. His cheeks were flushed, and his eyes were wild, and if I hadn't just come, the sight of him would have given me an instant erection.

"Come here." I held my hand out, and he shifted forwards. "Stand up."

When he climbed to his feet, I pressed him up against the wall and kissed him deeply, tasting myself on his tongue. He moaned as my hands went to his sweatpants, tugging them down. I ran my hand up and down his erection, trapped in his underwear, just as soaked as mine with the evidence of his arousal.

"Do you want me to take care of that?" I kissed his ear, his throat, his jaw, and finally his lips. His head falling forwards, he whispered, "Yes," into the crook of my neck, and I eased my hand inside his underwear, wrapping my fingers around his hardness. Another moan fell from his throat when I ran my thumb over the head of his cock, throbbing in my grip. It wouldn't take much for him to come all over my hand, and then I could make him lick it off.

Except...I wanted to taste him. Making a decision, I lowered myself to the floor, taking his underwear with me, and then closed my mouth around his cock.

JJ was delicious. Addictive. The perfect size to take into my mouth, to moan around his length, to drive him crazy until he spilled down my throat as I'd done to him.

I knew from our previous sexual encounter that he responded beautifully to something in his ass, and so I released him from my mouth. I soaked my finger in saliva and then dragged it across the head of his cock, getting it slippery wet. He moaned, his eyes rolling back as he planted one hand against the wall, the other sliding through my hair, not gripping but caressing, his nails a perfect pressure on my scalp. When I pressed my finger against his tight entrance, he shuddered, a gasping breath falling from his lips, and I smiled before taking him into my mouth again. It had been so long since I'd done this, but I couldn't ever remember being this into it before, let alone this focused on someone else's pleasure.

I pushed inside, encompassed by his heat, and he arched back, the fingers that had been sliding through my hair now gripping hard. He thrust his hips forwards, and I pulled back, placing a warning hand at the top of his thigh.

"Sorry. Too good," he breathed, and I smiled again. It wasn't that I minded him fucking my mouth, but it had been a long time, and the last thing I wanted was to make a fool of myself.

I drove my finger deeper as I sucked him harder. His thighs shook against my shoulders, bitten-off moans falling from his lips.

So beautiful.

"Gonna come," he panted, tightening his grip, and I pulled back, stroking him through his orgasm, closing my eyes as his cum hit my face. My own cock had recovered, hard and aching in my trousers, but I ignored it. I'd already come once tonight. All I wanted was to make sure he felt as good as I did.

Climbing to my feet, I made my way around my desk to the box of tissues and cleaned myself up, noticing him doing the same out of the corner of my eye. When I was finished, I met JJ's now-wary gaze. "What is it?"

He bit down on his lower lip. "What was the thing with you bringing me coffee all about?"

I shook my head, still no closer to an answer than I had been earlier. His brows pulled together, and he took a step back, rubbing his hand over his jaw. "Okay. I...I'm going to go now."

It was for the best, or so I told myself.

Tearing my gaze from him, and ignoring the part of me that was screaming, telling me I was making a mistake, I nodded. "I'll see you around."

"Killian?"

I glanced back up.

He hesitated, still worrying at his lip, and then he exhaled heavily. "The coffee has to stop. You know that, right?"

"I know. It was..." Fuck. "It'll stop."

With a nod, he swiped his bag from the floor, but he didn't make a move towards the door.

"What now?" I forced as much brusqueness into my voice as I could manage when he was staring at me with those pretty eyes.

"How often does this happen? The working too hard and forgetting to eat thing?"

I chuckled humourlessly. "It goes with the territory. You don't need to worry about me. I'm perfectly able to cope."

"Right." His eyes fluttered closed, his mouth turning downwards. When he opened them again, his gaze was impossible to read. "Want to swap numbers?"

Swapping numbers. No. That was a bad idea. Somehow, though, I found myself retrieving my phone from my desk drawer. Pausing for a moment, I met his gaze. "What would me giving you my number mean to you?"

He shrugged, shifting his bag on his shoulder with the movement. "It doesn't mean anything. We had fun. I'm not looking for anything. Fun is all I want. But...maybe if you're having a bad day, you could text me or something. I'm a good listener."

Right. I gave a brief nod. "Okay. Add your number. I'll text you...sometime."

A smile pulled at his lips, but it looked sad. He took my phone, tapping at the screen, and then slid it back across the table. "Done." Stepping back in a move reminiscent of the first time he'd been here, he opened the door. "Bye, Killian."

This routine was becoming far too familiar already. I hated it, because despite what my common sense told me, all I wanted was to keep him there with me.

I didn't want him to leave.

NINE

JJ

"You can do this."

Leo sucked in a shaky breath. "I don't think I can."

"You can, and you will," I promised him. "It's only my grandma and a few of her friends. You've got this. Just concentrate on the music and remember that you're not alone. Alyssa's here, and so am I. We've got this."

Trying to help Leo through his sometimes-crippling shyness was a relief, in a way. This was something I could deal with. A situation where I could be useful. Something that didn't involve a certain person who I'd given my phone number to and who hadn't sent a single text since.

Not to mention that on top of my other commitments, I also taught weekly dance classes to teenage students at a local youth centre. I was used to shyness, to anxiety, to debilitating nerves. This was something I was comfortable dealing with. I was in control.

Gently clasping Leo's chin, I forced him to look at me. "Place your hand on my chest." When his shaking fingers connected with my torso, I folded my free hand over his, holding it in place. "Good. Breathe, babe. Breathe with me."

When his eyes stopped looking so glassy and his breaths had slowed, I loosened my grip, giving him a reassuring smile. Performing for anyone was well out of his comfort zone. We'd become friends during an open day event that LSU had been hosting back when we were just prospective students. I'd been enthusing over the dance options on offer, deep in discussion with one of the current students, when I'd noticed a boy watching us, all huge green eyes and bright red hair, longing written all over his face. He was dressed in nondescript faded jeans, scuffed trainers, and a black T-shirt with a logo I couldn't identify, thanks to the course prospectus he had clutched to his chest.

The girl I'd been talking to noticed him watching us, and she beckoned him over with a friendly wave and a smile. His eyes had widened even further, if that was possible, and his cheeks had flushed a deep red. Shaking his head, he'd stammered something, backing away from us. I didn't know what it was, but some instinct had made me go to him, to take him aside into a quiet corner...

"S-sorry," he whispered, his chest rising and falling rapidly. "I-I didn't mean to stare."

"Nothing to apologise for. Are you interested in the dance degrees?"

He bit down on his lip. "I p-planned to do computing. But..."

"You get elective modules, right?" Tugging him over to a bench, I retrieved the brochures from his unresisting grip,

flipping through them. "Look, see. If you did this, or even this one, you'd need another fifteen-credit module to make up the right amount of credits for the first semester. Why don't you do dance? You can do whatever you want."

Staring at me, he whispered, "I can?"

"Yeah. You can. And from that look I saw on your face earlier, I think I have to insist that you do."

"You're...bossy," he said eventually, and I smiled.

"Better get used to it, babe. Because you and I are going to be friends."

Now, Leo was less shy and introverted than he had been when I first met him, at least with me, but it was always difficult to coax him out of his shell. He was so talented, though—not only at dance but with all his computing things that I barely understood. He'd never performed in front of an audience before, only as part of a group with just our instructors watching, and the way he'd been freaking out just having Killian watch a tiny part of our rehearsal had led me to take action.

So, here we were. At my grandma's retirement complex —where I occasionally ran impromptu casual dance lessons if I had some free time—ready to perform for a small number of residents and staff.

"Leo. You can do this," I repeated, and eventually, he gave me a jerky nod. With a final squeeze of his hand, I glanced over at Alyssa, and she turned to the sound system, fiddling with the buttons and dials before giving me a thumbs up. From her position in front and centre of the row of chairs that had been set out for our performance, G also gave me a thumbs up. I flashed her a grin as I took my place on the small stage area, which was simply a slightly raised wooden platform at the front of the room.

When the music began, I was instantly in the zone. I usually counted steps in my head—until the point they became so natural to me that I didn't even need to count—but today, I counted loud enough for Leo to hear, keeping him focused on the steps rather than our spectators. Out of the corner of my eye, I could see the minute it clicked for him, and he tuned the audience out, losing himself in the music. His body lost its stiffness, moving effortlessly between steps, and I allowed myself a small smile as we danced our way through the routine we'd choreographed together.

And then it was over. We'd made it all the way to the end of the routine. Taking a bow to the sound of applause from our tiny audience—and a loud whooping sound from my grandma—I grinned at my friends. There had been a few fumbles, but we had plenty of time to work on our issues before our showcase. This had been our first test run in front of an audience, and we'd made it through. I pulled Alyssa and Leo into a tight hug, the three of us breathless and laughing with that euphoric relief that comes from pulling off a complicated dance routine.

"I'm so fucking proud of you both." I pressed smacking kisses to their cheeks. "Look at how far we've come since the beginning of last semester."

"We did it!" Alyssa bounced on her toes, a blonde ball of energy. "I can't believe we did it!"

Leo shook his head in disbelief, a wide smile on his face. I didn't push him for words, knowing that after this, he'd need to retreat, to have some downtime alone to recover from the experience. But I could tell from the look on his face that he was happy, and that was all I wanted for him.

My grandma came over, and I introduced her to my friends. Once the introductions were out of the way, Leo quickly made his excuses and left while G talked Alyssa into joining me for an impromptu dance class with the residents. It mostly consisted of teaching a simple two-step routine and shuffling around the room, but everyone seemed to be enjoying themselves, and it made me smile.

When the class was over and Alyssa had left, I pulled on a hoodie and leg warmers to counteract the cooldown chill and grabbed my phone so I could take a quick selfie with G.

"Oh, Josh, that's a lovely photo." G studied the picture on my screen, smiling. Her finger flicked out, swiping back through my previous photos. I groaned internally, hoping I'd deleted anything incriminating.

"Is this your dance class?" She tapped on the screen on an image of my youth centre dance students, frozen in the midst of a routine.

"Yes." Prying my phone from her hands, I exited out of my gallery.

Then, my phone buzzed in my grip, and all thoughts of photos flew from my mind.

There was a text waiting for me.

UNKNOWN:

This is superior coffee. You should try it.
Far better for you than your overly-sweetened desserts attempting to pass as coffee

Beneath the message, there was an image of an ordinary, boring coffee. No pretty swirls of cream or sprinkles in sight. I immediately knew who it was. A smile tugged at my lips as I added his name to my contacts.

> **ME:**
>
> It's my only vice. Everything else I drink is healthy

My mind flew back to what had happened in his office, and without thinking it through, I hit Send on another text.

> **ME:**
>
> Especially when it comes directly from the source

A couple of aubergine and water emojis completed the message, and I grinned, already anticipating his reply.

> **KILLIAN:**
>
> I'm not even going to dignify that with a response

> **ME:**
>
> I bet you're thinking about what happened in your office aren't you?

> **KILLIAN:**
>
> JOSHUA JAMES

> **ME:**
>
> I love it when you full name me DOCTOR Wilder. Or would you prefer me to call you Sir?

> **KILLIAN:**
>
> Stop

ME:

No

KILLIAN:

Do not make me regret taking your number

ME:

You could never regret me

I tugged my lip between my teeth, replaying our recent interactions. I *hoped* he didn't, at least. Maybe I should ease up on the flirting, especially since this was the first time he'd texted me.

ME:

So tell me why you're sending me pics of your boring coffee and being incredibly insulting about my superior taste in coffee

KILLIAN:

I thought you should see what a proper coffee looks like

ME:

That's not coffee. That's tedium in a cup

"Josh?"

I lifted my head to find my grandma watching me, amusement in her gaze.

"Sorry. Sorry. Just...texting."

"Who's putting that smile on my boy's face? A new lover, perhaps?"

"G! I don't have lovers. That sounds so...old."

"Well, who is it? You wouldn't want to deprive your dear grandmother of the news, not when I'm on my deathbed." Her hand went to her forehead, and she pretended to swoon. I rolled my eyes.

"Deathbed, honestly. It's...he's a..." I paused. A friend didn't sound right because we barely knew each other. I definitely didn't want to tell her he was a lecturer at my university, and I absolutely was not going to tell her I'd— "He's a doctor," I finished. When her eyes widened, I shook my head. "Not a medical doctor. A doctor of something else. Don't ask me what because I'm not actually sure."

"Hmm. I think I'd like to meet this doctor." With a speed that belied her age, she snatched the phone from my hand, her gaze scanning my message thread with Killian.

"Give that back!"

"Just you wait a minute. Young people are so impatient," she tutted. My phone buzzed in her hand, and I groaned under my breath. Her brows furrowed as she jabbed at the screen, but her gaze cleared as she returned the phone to me, a smile tugging at her lips.

I didn't want to look.

When I lowered my gaze, I found a new reply from Killian that said, "Is that so?" and below that, G had replied *as me*, sending him my live fucking location, accompanied by a message that said, "I would like to try your tedious coffee."

"G! Wha—why would you do that? How did you even know how to do that?"

"I want to meet your doctor. And I may be old, but I'm not dead. They had a lovely young gentleman come to teach us how to do all sorts of things with our telephones a few weeks ago. Jason, his name was. Lovely manners."

"He's not my doctor. And he's not coming here, so get that idea out of your head."

Except...I hadn't read the latest reply from Killian.

Three words.

On my way.

"Oh, my. Josh. You didn't tell me your doctor was so handsome." My grandma batted her wispy lashes at a visibly disconcerted Killian—that was, until his expression shuttered.

She was right, though. He was very fucking handsome. He looked hot as fuck in the suits and smart clothes he wore for work, but today, he'd gone casual with dark-blue jeans that hugged his legs, polished tan loafers, and a forest-green soft knitted jumper that somehow enhanced his light eyes. He'd pushed up the sleeves, and seeing those strong forearms with his dark hair and those capable hands with the knuckles flexing was making my mind go in directions that were very inappropriate when one's grandmother was in the same room.

Killian rubbed a hand over the stubble of his jaw, his gaze sliding to mine before going back to my grandma. He cleared his throat, clearly wondering why on earth I'd invited him here—which I hadn't. Thanks, G.

I sighed. "G. Stop making this weird. I can't take you anywhere." Tucking my arm through hers, I faced Killian. "I guess it's down to me to make the introductions. Grandma, this is Killian. Killian, this is my grandma, Glynis."

Killian's face remained impassive, but I could see the muscle ticking in his jaw. I didn't blame him. Having him meet the woman who raised me was not something I'd ever expected to happen, and I was at as much of a loss as he was. She knew some of my friends, sure—Niccolò was her favourite—but she'd never met any of the men I'd slept with.

He recovered quickly, though. "Glynis. It's a pleasure." Gently clasping her hand, he lifted it to his lips, and something inside me warmed. "If I'd have known I was going to meet you—in fact, please excuse me for a moment." He backed away from us and disappeared out of the door. As soon as he was gone, I turned to my grandma.

"I can't believe you did that! What's he going to think? He thinks I invited him here to meet you, and he's not—we're not like that! He's—he's—"

"Don't get so worked up, dear." She patted my arm. "I saw the way he looked at you when he walked in."

"How did he look at me?"

A soft, indulgent smile curved over her lips. "It was as if no one else existed in that moment. You were all he saw."

I shook my head with a disbelieving laugh. G saw what she wanted to see. "He didn't look at me like that."

She ignored my comment, instead looking towards the door that Killian had disappeared through. "Another older man, hmm? You do seem to gravitate towards them, or so Niccolò tells me."

That little fucker. "G."

Her humour died away. "You know age is nothing but a number, darling. Your grandad was thirteen years older than me."

"I know that, and I know you don't care about age. But that's not what this is, okay? Killian only came because he was being polite."

"Hmm. We'll see," was all she said. I managed to

change the subject to the latest gossip in the retirement complex, and the interrogation was dropped. For now.

When Killian returned a short while later, he cleared his throat as he stopped in front of G, producing a bouquet of flowers in whites and yellows and oranges from behind his back. "Beautiful flowers for a beautiful lady," he said, presenting the bouquet to my grandma with a flourish. My heart skipped a beat at seeing this man—who I now knew had such a thoughtful side—effortlessly charming my grandma. How and where he'd managed to get them so quickly, I had no idea, nor why he'd even thought to do so, but the delight in G's face brought a lump to my throat.

Thanks, I mouthed as my grandma motioned for him to stoop so she could press a kiss to his cheek. He flushed, glancing over at me before returning his attention to G, but there was a smile tugging at the corners of his lips.

I didn't get a chance to say anything more to him because my grandma immediately beckoned one of the staff members over, asking them for some water and a vase for the flowers "this wonderful gentleman" had brought for her. When the flowers had been dealt with, G turned on the charm, somehow managing to find out more about Killian in a few minutes than I'd found out in all our interactions together. Some of it I knew already, but some of the information was new.

Dr. Killian Wilder. Thirty years old, with a PhD in business management. No close family and had lived alone since the age of seventeen. A principal lecturer who was hoping to gain a professorship and become the head of LSU's business school.

He answered my grandma's questions with endless

patience, even though it was clear that he was uncomfortable with being put on the spot. G eventually noticed my discreet hand and eye signals and excused herself.

When she was gone, Killian glanced over at me. "Can I have a word?"

I followed him to a quiet corner of the room. He stopped and stared down at me, a rare hesitance in his eyes. His fingers lightly curled around my bicep, and I inhaled sharply, goosebumps spreading over my skin at his touch. The way this man affected me was like nothing else.

"I want to speak to you privately, if that's acceptable to you."

"Yeah, of course that's acceptable. Where? There's a café just down the road."

"No. Private." The way he emphasised "private" made my eyes widen. "Do you want to come to mine when you've finished here? My flat's close by."

Did I want to see the space that Dr. Killian Wilder called his home? Yes, yes, I did.

"Okay. I'll probably stay another half an hour or so, but I could come after that?"

Killian nodded. "Take as long as you need. I'll text you the address."

TEN

JJ

I glanced around me, taking in Killian's flat. It was an open-plan space on the top floor of a Victorian building, with battered original wooden floorboards and walls painted in a soft, creamy grey. The kitchen area was more modern, with pale grey polished stone worktops and glossy blue cupboards, and there was a leather sofa and a large armchair at the far end of the space in front of a TV and sound system. It was gorgeous, but as I looked around, I couldn't help feeling as if it was staged, like no one really lived inside. There were no photos. No ornaments or books cluttering the shelves, other than a hefty business studies hardcover on the wooden coffee table that looked as if it could double up as a weapon.

"This is nice."

"Joshua."

"Yeah?" I turned to see Killian casually leaning against the wall, his arms folded across his chest. My heart beat faster.

"I didn't invite you here to admire the decor."

"No?" I took a step towards him, then another. His gaze darkened, turning hungry as he raked it all over me, leaving me feeling exposed and completely fucking breathless. My own gaze dropped from his face to the large bulge between his legs, trapped within the jeans I wanted to peel from his strong thighs. Fuck. I needed him again. This was becoming an obsession, and I wasn't sure how I felt about that.

But I couldn't resist him.

"No," he confirmed, a dark smile on his lips. "Come here."

When I was right in front of him, he unfolded his arms.

"Do you know what I thought when I saw you in those shorts and leg warmers, even with this monstrosity—" He plucked at one of the strings of my cerise hoodie. "—covering the best parts?"

"No." Placing my hand on his chest, I pressed my hips into his. I wanted him so badly. "But you're going to tell me."

"Yes, I am." He lowered his head, his mouth going to my ear. "I thought you looked. So. Fucking. Sexy." He punctuated each word with a nip to the shell of my ear, his hot breath sending tingles across my skin. "All I could think about was doing this."

His mouth went to my throat, his hand gripping my jaw and tilting my head to the side. He kissed down the side of my neck and then let go of me. But only for a second. He curved his fingers around the hem of my hoodie and lifted it over my head, leaving me in my microfibre black dance shorts, baby blue leg warmers, and a matching blue T-shirt that was cropped just above my navel.

A groan fell from Killian's lips as his gaze seared me. "Fucking hell, Joshua. You make my dick so fucking hard."

My stomach flipped, and my dick jerked. "Kiss me. Please." I cupped the back of his neck, pulling him forwards, and then we were kissing, properly kissing, mouths and tongues meeting over and over again, hot and so fucking frantic as we raced to divest ourselves and each other of enough of our clothes that we could fuck. Killian lifted me into his arms, not breaking our kiss as he staggered over to the sofa. It was a blur of hands and mouths and his hard body against mine, and then he was opening me up, producing a condom and lube from nowhere as he plunged his fingers in and out of me, readying me for his cock in record time. I panted against his throat as he gripped my hips, angling me the way he wanted me, and then I was finally sinking down onto his big, thick erection.

"Oh, fuck. Finally," I moaned, my head falling back as he sucked a bruise into my chest. I'd get questions about it, but I couldn't bring myself to care. I wanted his marks on me.

"You feel so fucking good around my cock. So fucking tight and hot." He thrust up as I thrust down. "I want to fuck you so hard."

"Do it. Please," I panted. "Fuck me so good that I can still feel you tomorrow."

With a growl, he lifted me off him and manhandled me onto my knees, facing the back of the sofa, my hands clasping the backrest. Without any warning, he tugged my thighs farther apart and then plunged back inside. We both groaned as he fucked me hard and fast, so deep and so good, his cock at the perfect angle to make me see stars.

"I'm so close." Fuck. He felt incredible. I couldn't get enough.

"Come for me, Joshua," he commanded in a low rasp, and that did it. My cock jerked, shooting all over the back of his leather sofa, pumping out my release, completely untouched.

"Your turn to come for me, Dr. Wilder," I rasped with what remained of my breath.

"*Fuck*," he ground out, his hips slamming into me as his cock pulsed inside me, filling the condom with his cum. I collapsed forwards, my forehead landing on the cool leather of the sofa back, and he came with me, panting into my ear as he wrapped his arm around my waist. Our bodies were overheated and slick with sweat, but neither of us attempted to move.

"You liked it when I called you Dr. Wilder, hmm?" I eventually managed to breathe out shakily.

He chuckled against my nape, pressing a kiss to my skin. "It's a first for me, I have to say."

The thought of being the first *anything* for him was something that I enjoyed far too much. I wasn't sure if I liked the way I was rapidly becoming addicted to this man, a problem he seemed to share based on recent events.

I changed the subject before I could dwell on it any further. "I don't think I can get up. You fucked all my energy out of me."

His smile curved over my skin. "I suppose I'll have to replenish your energy, won't I? If...if you want to stay."

"I want to stay."

ELEVEN

JJ

Curled up on the now-clean sofa, dressed in my oversized hoodie, fresh pale blue boxer briefs, and the pair of thigh-high blue fluffy socks I always kept in my dance bag, I ran a hand through my hair. It was still damp from the shower I'd taken, and I hoped it wasn't too much of a mess. Adjusting my reading glasses on my nose, I attempted to concentrate on the book in front of me. The soft creak of the floorboards alerted me to Killian's presence as I pulled the instrument of torture closer. When I was sure he could hear my words without me raising my voice, I tapped the cover of the book.

"You know, you could use this as a weapon if anyone breaks in. Swing it at their head—it'd be enough to knock anyone out."

Silence.

I raised my head to find a freshly showered Killian, dressed in low-slung, soft grey pyjama trousers and a black T-shirt that stretched across his torso, staring at me. He was completely still, his gaze focused on my legs.

"What? Oh. Is it the socks?" I extended one of my legs in front of me, stroking over the fluffy texture. "I always carry a pair in my dance bag. I prefer them to my leg warmers, but they're too thick to wear with my trainers."

"It's not the socks," he muttered. "It's...it's..." Trailing off, he rubbed his hand across his face. "You look so... *comfortable*. So at home. In *my* home."

Oh. "Is it making you uncomfortable? I can leave. Honestly, I won't be offen—"

"No. Don't leave." Finally springing into action, he came over to the sofa, laying a heavy hand on my shoulder and leaning down to press a hard kiss to the top of my head. This was new, and it gave me a weird, tickly feeling in my stomach. "Stay. I want you to stay."

"Then I'll stay." Tilting my head back so I could meet his gaze, I let the truth fall from my lips. "This is weird for me, too, you know. I'm normally more of a fuck-and-duck, if you know the term. I don't hang around."

He grimaced. "Not that one-night stands feature very frequently in my life, but it's the same for me, too." His thumb was stroking small circles into my shoulder as he spoke, and I wasn't sure he was even aware of it. "Relationships aren't for me—" He broke off, his eyes widening along with mine as the R-word hung in the air between us. "That wasn't what I meant. I simply meant that I don't invite people into my home. Yet you somehow make me break all my rules."

"We don't have to make this into a big deal. It's just, y'know, friends hanging out together."

A humourless smile tugged at his lips. "Friends. Is that

even possible? We're so different, and you're...you're a student. I'm a decade older than you, Joshua."

"Oh, fuck that." Ripping off my glasses and throwing them on the coffee table, I leapt off the sofa, storming around to face him and jabbing a finger into his chest. "So what if we're different? You don't get to play that age card with me. Do you know who my best friend is? My grandma. She's eighty-two, Kill. Do you think that's wrong?"

A muscle ticked in his jaw as he stared me down. "It's not the same. There's an imbalance of power here."

"How is there? Okay, you teach at the uni. So what? You don't teach *me*. There's no conflict of interest here."

"It's not—"

"If you're looking for an excuse to change your mind or you want me to leave, just say it. I don't like games. I prefer to be upfront so everyone knows what's going on."

"Fuck," he growled and yanked me to him, slamming his lips down on mine. The kiss turned from hard to soft after only a few seconds, his arms winding around me as he licked along the seam of my lips, taking small, nipping kisses until I opened my mouth for him, his tongue sliding against mine. When we broke apart, he exhaled heavily. "Fuck. Forget what I said. I want you to stay. Come on. Take a seat at the island while I cook. That way, I can't see your tempting fucking legs in those socks."

"Ah, you do like the socks." I grinned at him, and he nipped at my lip, swatting my ass.

"Behave. You know what you look like, and you know you make my cock hard. No more distracting me, or you won't get any dinner."

"Yes, sir." I batted my lashes at him, and he spun me

around, yanking me back against his chest and holding me in place, one arm banded around my waist and the other hand wrapped around my throat. His huge erection was pressed into me, and his breath was hot on my ear.

"None of that. My house, my rules. You do as I say, or there will be consequences. Do I make myself clear?"

My dick was so. Fucking. Hard.

"Yes, Dr. Wilder."

"You little—" He didn't even bother to complete the sentence, yanking my boxer briefs down, bending me back over the sofa, and after rolling on another condom, he fucked me hard for the second time in the space of an hour, leaving me breathless and shaky-legged.

When we were both cleaned up again, I gingerly took a seat on one of the cushioned stools at the kitchen island, sore in the best way. He caught my wince and smirked at me.

"Feeling a little sore?"

"Well, you did fuck me twice in an hour, and your dick's on the large side. I'm going to be feeling it tomorrow."

"Good." His smirk curved into a satisfied smile, but then he frowned, turning away from me and rummaging in one of the kitchen cupboards. He pulled out a small cardboard packet and slid it across the island to me. "Take two ibuprofen. It'll help to ease any inflammation. You can...you can have a bath if you like. I'm sorry. I should've offered."

Warmth spread through my chest as I opened the ibuprofen packet, popping two pills from the blister pack and swallowing them with the glass of water he'd placed in front of me. Having someone taking care of me after sex was new and definitely not unwelcome. I guess we were both going through a number of firsts today. "Thanks. I'll be okay, though."

"Alright." He paused. "But...if you change your mind, you know where the bathroom is." Killian's expression had shuttered, and I knew that if he was feeling anything like I was, this weird level of domesticity we'd somehow slipped into had to be scaring him, at least a bit.

I nodded, keeping my tone light. "Come on, then. Impress me with your cooking skills. What are we having?"

He crossed to his fridge, examining the contents. "Any allergies? Any foods you dislike?"

"No, and no."

"Good." Pulling out ingredients, he assembled them on the island. "How competent are you in the kitchen?"

That raised brow he directed at me did things to me. "Excuse me, Dr. Wilder. I'll have you know G taught me to cook at a very young age. I did a lot of the cooking for us until we moved out of our house, in fact."

"Is that so? In that case, you can chop these peppers."

I sighed, shaking my head. "If I'd known you were inviting me here to be your unpaid prep chef, I might've said no."

His eyes lit up with amusement, and fucking hell, this man was doing things to me. Things I didn't know how to deal with.

Placing down the kitchen knife he'd been holding, he rounded the island, coming up behind me and planting his hands on the counter on either side of my body, caging me in. He dipped his head to my ear. "I'd say you've been fairly compensated so far, wouldn't you?"

Leaning back slightly so that my back pressed against

his chest, I sighed again. "That was mutually beneficial. I'm sorry, but it doesn't count."

"Greedy boy," he murmured, trailing his nose down the side of my cheek. "Always wanting more."

Fuck, my dick was responding to him like I hadn't just come twice in an hour. "You're no better."

One of his hands came up to cup my jaw, tilting my head to the side. His teeth nipped at the side of my throat, and then he kissed me. I shivered against him. "You're the most tempting fucking thing I've ever had the pleasure of having in my flat, but how about an IOU? We both need to eat."

The most tempting. I was feeling far too happy with all these firsts. Why was this so easy between us? It was so unexpected.

"I suppose that'll do." I twisted on the stool. "Kiss me, and then we'll cook."

Killian's thumb stroked my jaw as his lips met mine, softly and far too quickly. When he stepped back, his pupils were blown wide, his gaze hungry, and I fucking ached for him.

"Don't look at me like that, Joshua." As if he wasn't the one looking at me like he wanted to devour me. "We need to eat."

When he was back on the other side of the island, I could breathe again, concentrating on the process of methodically cutting the peppers into long, even slices.

"You used to do a lot of the cooking?"

I glanced up at Killian. He had his back to me, tipping ingredients into a large wok on the hob. "Yeah. It was just the two of us, and I wanted to help my grandma. She was...unconventional, I guess, keeping odd hours and having friends over all the time. She let me invite mine, too. Our house was open to everyone. But when I was at school, obviously, I had to stick to a schedule, and so I did a lot of the cooking. I ate when I needed to eat, and I always made sure I cooked enough for her, too, so she could have it whenever it suited her. On Sunday mornings, she used to do a huge breakfast for everyone who'd stayed over, and those were probably my favourite times. We'd put on one of her old records, and she'd tell me wild stories—half of which had no basis in reality—and dance me around the kitchen in between cooking mounds of bacon and eggs and whatever else we had in the cupboards."

"That sounds nice." There was a note of wistfulness in Killian's tone.

"It was." I smiled to myself. "I'm lucky to have her. She's one in a million."

"It was clear to me how much you mean to each other when I saw you both together today. When did the two of you move away from each other?"

"It wasn't long after I finished school. G was beginning to struggle with everyday tasks, and I was doing everything I could, but I was worrying about her every time I left the house. A couple of her friends had moved into the retirement complex—it had only just opened, and they were raving about the facilities and the social calendar. It piqued her interest, so we went to look around it, and we both fell in love with it. She rented out the house because neither of us could bear to sell it, I found a student house share, and we've been in the same places ever since."

Killian turned to face me, his gaze searching. I steeled myself, but all he said was, "Time to add the peppers."

Swinging my legs off the stool, I padded around the island to him, carefully adding the peppers into the stir-fry mix. Before I could move away, he wrapped his fingers around my wrist, stopping me in my tracks.

"Do you miss living with her?"

Allowing myself to briefly lean into his warmth, I nodded. "I do. I know it's for the best, and we both keep busy, and we see each other as often as we can, but…"

He didn't respond, but he squeezed my wrist gently before releasing.

"Why did you come today? Why did you text me about the coffee?" The questions spilled out of me, hanging in the air between us. There was silence for a long moment, but eventually, he huffed out a breath, shaking his head.

"Honestly? I don't have an answer I can give you. I…I sent you the coffee text. Then I saw your text inviting me to join you—or what I thought was your text. I'm assuming from the shock on your face when I walked in that you weren't the sender. Anyway, I read the text, and before I knew it, I'd deviated from my usual walking route and ended up outside the retirement complex."

"G sent it," I confirmed, and then added, "but I'm glad you came, just so you know."

"Me too," he murmured, so quietly that I could barely hear him.

I remained silent while the stir-fry cooked, and only after we'd finished eating did I dare to bring up the subject I was most curious about.

"You told G you'd lived alone since you were seventeen."

In the middle of loading the dishwasher, Killian paused, his shoulders stiffening. "I did. Don't try and give me sympathy. Not all foster parents have their foster kids' best interests at heart, but it was much better than some of the alternatives. I've been lucky."

I wanted to ask more, but the set of his shoulders told me that anything else I mentioned would be unwelcome. Why was it so important that I learned more about him, anyway? What was it about this man, living here alone in this beautiful but sterile flat, that made me want to stay when I never had before?

"Okay. What about being a lecturer? Do you enjoy that? You want to be the head of the department, right? How does that happen?"

I could see him visibly relax, and I breathed out a shaky breath, crossing over to the fridge to refill our wine glasses with the bottle he'd opened when we ate. As I was pouring, he straightened up, closing the dishwasher and setting it to run. His gaze drifted to me, then to the wine glasses, and a half-smile tugged at his lips.

"Making yourself at home, I see."

"Yeah."

"Come on, then. Bring the wine over to the sofa, and I suppose we can talk, if we must."

"That was why you invited me here, wasn't it? That's what you said earlier."

He laughed darkly, swiping his glass from the counter and bending his head to my ear as he did so. "We both know I didn't invite you here to talk, Joshua."

Fuck. It was like he had a direct line to my dick. One minute, I was trying to have a conversation; the next, I was struggling to remember what words even were.

But he stepped away, moving to the seating area and sinking into the large armchair to the left of the sofa. When he'd placed his wine glass on the coffee table, he lifted a brow, and I went to him, settling on the sofa with my wine glass in hand. I did my best to ignore the impulse to straddle Killian's thighs and kiss him, instead staring into my wine glass as he began to speak.

"I'm good at my job. I work hard at it. It's always been my plan to become the head of the school of business. That would be the pinnacle of my career, and to be able to do it at my age would be unprecedented. The process isn't the same everywhere, but at LSU, faculty members are usually promoted to a professorship and the role of department head when an opening becomes available or if someone proves to be unfit for the role. They're chosen by a committee headed up by the vice chancellor of LSU."

"So there's an opening?" I prompted when he fell silent.

He nodded slowly. "There is...or will be. The current head is retiring next year, and so the role will become available. I-I want it. I'm just...I'm not sure if I'll get it."

"Why wouldn't you? You're already the principal lecturer. Surely it makes sense."

Picking up his wine glass, he shook his head. "Unfortunately, that's only part of it. The committee looks more favourably on faculty members who are...let's say... socially involved. I...well, socialising isn't my strong point, in case you hadn't guessed, nor do I want it to be. There are other members of staff who are far more suited to the position when that's taken into account."

Oh. My mind flashed back to Killian, alone in his office in front of his computer, with tired eyes and stiff shoulders and a forgotten sandwich discarded on the side of his desk. Then to his words earlier, *I've lived alone since I was seventeen*, and then to his flat that wasn't a home.

I'd once told my friends I was like their fairy godmother. Maybe that was why this man had been put in my life, because he needed that from me, too.

"You know, I'm pretty social. If you want anyone to, uh, go through things with, I could be there for you. If you wanted."

When I chanced a look at him, he was staring, unseeing, at the wall, his hand clenched around the stem of his wine glass and his jaw set.

"Kill?"

He sighed heavily. "There's a spring faculty dinner and dance coming up, and based on the way my colleagues talk about it, it's the social event of the year. I've never attended before, but my colleague Gage has encouraged me to attend this year. He thinks it'll earn me socialisation points if I can get my shit together and actually socialise for once—his words, not mine."

"I think I need to meet this Gage. He sounds like he knows what he's talking about." I shot Killian a teasing grin, but it was the wrong thing to say because his brows pulled together, and he gave a sharp jerk of his head.

"No. Fraternising with students is not going to help my agenda."

Fuck. I knew he was right, but—

He slammed his wine glass down onto the table, making liquid slosh over the edge, and before I had time to blink, he was crouching in front of me, his big hands on my thighs, gazing up at me through his thick lashes.

"I'm sorry. I didn't mean to snap at you."

I was momentarily speechless. Meeting his eyes, I lifted my hand, cupping the side of his face, feeling the roughness of his stubble against my palm. When I'd gathered my thoughts, I stroked my fingers through his hair in a gesture that appeared to calm him and therefore me. "I meant what I said. I could help you out if you wanted me to. If this dinner is important for your chances of promotion, then we should give you the best chance possible, right?"

He sighed. "I guess it couldn't hurt. Seems a bit strange, though, doesn't it? I should be the one with my shit together. I'm the teacher, and you're the student."

If he brought up my age again... "Even teachers still need to learn, Kill. Sooner or later, you're gonna have to face the fact that there are some things I'm naturally proficient in, and I might just be able to teach you a thing or two."

His hands slid up my bare legs, stopping at my boxer briefs. "And what do you get out of it?" One finger traced a circle on my inner thigh.

I swallowed, my cock reacting to the feel of his hands on my skin. "Access to the hottest fucking doctor I've ever seen," I said hoarsely, my words ending on a gasp when he slid his hand directly onto my cock, pressing lightly down with his palm.

"Such a greedy boy. Always wanting more. When will you be satisfied?" he murmured, rubbing his thumb across my cockhead, my precum dampening the fabric. *Fuck.*

"When will you be?" Lifting my leg, I ran my foot over the tent in his trousers. He swore under his breath, palming me harder, my cock jerking beneath his touch.

I tugged at his hair. "Stop fucking teasing me and make me come."

"So demanding." But he pulled off my hoodie, allowing us both a full view of the effect he had on me.

"Look at you," he rasped, his gaze drinking me in, hot and hungry. "Fuck, Joshua. *Fuck*."

The way he was looking at me. It was almost too much. "Killian. Please come here."

Standing up, he tugged down his pyjama trousers, allowing me to see the mouthwatering sight of his thick cock, hard and ready for me. He pushed me back so I was lying lengthways on the sofa, yanked off my underwear, and then crawled on top of me. I wrapped my legs around him, closing my eyes as I ran my hands up and down the powerful lines of his back. Neither of us said anything more, moving against each other almost desperately until first I came, and then he did, our combined release smearing messily between us.

I had a sinking feeling that my answer to his earlier question, *When will you be satisfied?* was at best *not yet* and at worst *never*.

Either answer scared me.

TWELVE

KILLIAN

I stepped into the lecture theatre, and silence fell immediately. Planting my hands on either side of the lectern, I stared my students down. Some shifted in their seats, unease on their faces, while others—

Fucking Loveridge.

"Loveridge!" I barked.

His head shot up, and he smirked at me. "Yes, sir?"

Arrogant little fuck.

"Mr. Holmes' head is not a wastepaper basket."

"Yeah, Ander." Liam Holmes, now wearing a matching smirk, picked up the balled-up piece of paper that had landed on his table, throwing it back in the direction of Ander Loveridge.

"Enough," I ground out, and fucking finally, their smirks disappeared. "Would anyone else like to waste more time, or can we get on with today's seminar? You're paying for the privilege of being here. Remember that."

"Grumpy fucker," someone muttered from the front row, which stopped me in my tracks. The front row was where the students who actually wanted to be here chose to sit, generally. Was I really—

Shit. JJ's face appeared in my mind, the sincerity in his gaze when he'd offered to help me with my social skills... and, well, he had a point.

I exhaled heavily. Maybe if I imagined he was here, I could do this. Be...nicer. "Alright. Last week, we looked at outsourcing non-core business functions. Today, I'd like to look at insourcing non-core business functions, and then I want you to get into small groups of three or four and discuss the strengths and weaknesses of each approach. If there's something you're unsure about after I've been through today's material, you can come and see me, and I'll be—" Fuck. Just say it. "—happy to answer your questions."

A shocked silence followed my words. I glanced at Ander Loveridge, who was staring at me with his mouth wide open and his brows at his hairline. It took all my self-restraint to keep from making a cutting remark, but by keeping my jaw clenched shut and thinking of JJ, I managed. How on earth did my sunshine boy live with such an irritating man-child?

No. JJ wasn't "my" anything. This agreement between us was temporary, and as soon as the faculty dinner was out of the way, we'd go our separate ways.

***

"Uh. Dr. Wilder." Tearing my gaze away from my laptop, I glanced up from my position behind the desk next to the lectern to see Ander Loveridge standing in front of me.

"Yes, Mr. Loveridge? What can I help you with?"

"The thing you said about TUPE law—I'm not sure if I understood it properly. It's gonna be in my assignment, isn't it?"

I sighed inwardly but nodded towards the spare chair in the corner of the room. "Pull up a chair, and we'll go through it."

He stared at me, open-mouthed, for the second time in an hour. I rolled my eyes.

"Go."

"Okay. Yeah. I'll. Okay." Finally, he moved, dragging the chair back over as I scrolled through my lecture notes to the relevant section.

"Make a note of this. Page 203 in your textbook. Read it. Then read it again. Then summarise it with bullet points."

"Now? You want me to email it to you, or—"

"No, and no. Read and summarise in your own time. I don't need to see it. You're an intelligent man, Mr. Loveridge, when you apply yourself."

"I've heard that before," he mumbled, and I almost smiled. Almost.

"Perhaps you should listen to the advice. Right, can you see my screen? I want you to focus on this chart..."

To my surprise and his, he gave me his full attention and even asked a number of insightful questions as I spoke. When I'd finished going through the material and I was sure he'd grasped it, he cleared his throat.

"Dr. Wilder? Sorry for earlier. I was getting Liam back for this morning—"

I held up my hand, cutting him off. "I don't want to

know. But I accept your apology. And please, don't call me Dr. Wilder."

"Huh?"

Fuck. Why had those words slipped out?

JJ. Again. The thought of him calling me Dr. Wilder in that sexy-as-fuck, sultry tone...

"Call me sir. Maybe one day, you'll even earn the right to call me by my first name."

Again, he gaped at me. "Fucking hell. What's happening here? Have I been dropped into a parallel universe or something? Are you feeling okay?"

And just like that, he was back to his usual irritating self.

"Get out of my sight, Loveridge."

"Yes, sir." Shooting to his feet, he saluted me, a grin curving over his lips. "Thanks again for the help."

When he was gone, I realised that I'd returned his smile.

Fuck.

ME:

I had an interesting conversation with your housemate this morning

JJ:

Which one? Was it about me? It's all lies I swear

ME:

Ha ha. Ander Loveridge. I have you to
thank for my restraint. I spent the last
quarter of his seminar giving him a one to
one lesson on TUPE law

JJ:

I have no idea what TUPE is but I'm proud
of myself for being the reason for your
restraint. And proud of you too, I guess

ME:

Transfer of Undertakings (Protection of
Employment) Regulations

JJ:

Shouldn't that be TUPER?

ME:

Not the point, Joshua. Pay attention

JJ:

I love it when you get bossy, Dr. Wilder. Are
you free today? I had an idea for something
you could try out for your social skills

ME:

Come to my office at 4. Don't be late

JJ:

Yes sir

He sent a GIF of someone saluting, and for a moment, it was far too close to Loveridge's actions for my liking. Shaking off the thought, I returned my attention to my lesson planning. The vice chancellor wanted me to join the rest of the business school faculty in delivering some of my lectures online—prerecording them for students to watch at their own convenience. So far, I'd resisted. One, I liked to see the reactions of my students in real time. Two, I was of the belief that if they were paying good money to be here on campus, we should offer them face-to-face teaching. No doubt, teaching online would make things less stressful for me, but I could envision my emails increasing rapidly, with students asking inane questions that could easily be answered in a minute or two during the lecture. I had the feeling that I wouldn't be able to avoid it forever, though, not if I wanted to be seen as a team player.

Caught up in my lesson plans, I lost track of time, startling out of my thoughts at a knock at the door. I glanced at my watch. Four o'clock already. A smile tugged at my lips, my fatigue melting away.

"Come in."

The door swung open.

"Wow. You hardly ever look this pleased to see me." Gage strode into the room, perching on the corner of my desk. Fuck. He raised a brow. "What's with the good mood?"

The smile slid from my face. "Nothing. I'm not in a good mood."

Gage's reply died in his throat when we both heard the soft tap at the door. He glanced at the door, and then at me, and then back to the door. "Who could it be?" Before I could do or say anything, he swung himself off the desk, strode over to the door, and threw it open. "Hello, there."

There was a moment of silence, and then I heard JJ's voice. "Hi."

This was going to be a fucking disaster.

"Come in." Gage swept his arm out. "I assume you're here to see the good doctor Killian?"

JJ shot me a cautious glance, but when I said nothing—

because how the fuck was I supposed to react in this situation?—he treated Gage to one of his sunshine smiles. "I am. I don't think I've had the pleasure. I'm JJ, and you are…"

"Gage."

"Oh, *Gage.*"

I pinched my brow. Now Gage would know—

Gage's brows flew up, his eyes widening, but he recovered quickly. "He's mentioned me to you, has he? Now I'm at a disadvantage because Kill likes to play his cards close to his chest, and he never tells *me* anything." My annoying colleague directed a poor attempt at a wounded look at me, complete with a pout that he absolutely couldn't pull off. "Tell me about yourself. You look familiar. Have we met before? You're not in any of my classes, are you?"

Shit. The club. If Gage put two and two together, he'd make five.

"JJ's studying for a BA in dance. You've probably seen him around the campus." Sudden panic made the words trip off my tongue.

But Gage wasn't satisfied, his brows creasing as he eyed JJ with suspicion. "Dance? This is the business school."

JJ's gaze slid to mine and then back to Gage. "I'm the housemate of one of Killian's students. You know his reputation for terrorising his poor victims. I like to think of myself as a go-between. I drop my housemate's assignments off when Killian scares him into delivering them personally rather than being satisfied with the online portal like every other lecturer." His voice was teasing, and Gage responded with a loud bark of laughter.

"I like you already. Since you're not one of Kill's

students, how would you feel about being recruited to my mission?"

"Mission?"

"To make Kill socialise more."

"Gage," I cautioned. "JJ isn't here for that." Hopefully, he wouldn't realise that I was lying through my teeth.

"Nope. This is perfect, if you think about it. He can give you a student's perspective, and I think you could do with that. Don't forget your two-year plan."

Dropping my head to my desk, I groaned. "Fuck off. Please."

"Uh. Okay."

"Not you." Without lifting my head from my desk, I jabbed my index finger in the approximate direction of my annoying colleague. "You."

"Okay, okay. I'll go. I know when I'm not wanted. But just so you're aware, this conversation isn't over." Footsteps sounded, then stopped. "I almost forgot why I came in here. Stuart and his wife are organising a small thing on Friday with a few of the other faculty members. It's casual, just drinks at a bar. You're coming."

"No."

"Yes. Kill, come on. Remember your plan."

"If I say I'll think about it, will you leave me alone?"

"If you say yes, I'll leave right now."

"Fine. *Yes.* Now kindly fuck off."

I heard footsteps again, followed by the soft creak of the door closing. When I judged Gage had finally gone far enough away, I raised my head from the desk, rubbing the spot between my brows.

"Sorry." JJ bit down on his lip, his gaze dropping to the

floor. "I wasn't sure how you wanted me to act or what Gage knew already. I hope I didn't make anything too awkward for you."

Extending my hand, I shook my head. "Come here."

When he reached me, I gripped his wrist, pulling him down to straddle my thighs. Lifting my hands, I gently tugged his lip from between his teeth, smoothing my thumb across his soft skin. He exhaled, giving me a hesitant smile.

"You didn't do anything wrong. Gage caught me by surprise, too. He's...he'll be like a dog with a bone now, though, just to warn you." Leaning forwards, I did what I'd been dreaming of since the last time I'd seen JJ. I kissed those delicious plush lips, feeling them curve into a proper smile beneath my touch.

"Hi," he said when he drew back.

"Hi. Have you had a good day? Drink any more overpriced sugary desserts?"

His smile widened, his eyes sparkling as he slid his hands onto my shoulders. "Drink any more soulless brews? My day was good, yeah. We nailed the section of the choreography I'd been worrying about, and—"

"Fuck, you're gorgeous." *I missed you.* I captured his lips again, coaxing his mouth open with my tongue. It was risky because my door wasn't locked, and I wouldn't put it past Gage to barge in again, but I couldn't hold back from kissing JJ. It felt as necessary as breathing.

Eventually pulling away from him, although it was the last thing I wanted, I stroked my fingers through the waves of his hair, pushing it back from his face. Inside, a part of me was demanding to know what I was doing, because in the thirty years I'd been alive, I'd never once done this. Never caressed someone just because I wanted to and I knew they'd enjoy the feeling, too. But it was as if my hands had a mind of their own. My other was holding his waist, my thumb lightly rubbing over his hip bone, and even my confusion at my own actions didn't stop me.

"Tell me more about your choreography while I finish up here."

One brow rose, his gaze searching mine. "Do you really want to know, or are you just being polite?"

"I want to know." I did. I wanted to know because it was important to him, and honestly, that fucking scared me.

As I put the finishing touches on the final slide of my lesson plan, saved my work, and then shut everything down, JJ described to me how he'd reworked a part of the choreography for his group showcase dance with Alyssa and Leo and how it had all come together today. While I didn't understand the technicalities of what he was telling me, I got the general gist. Seeing his face light up as he spoke just highlighted how passionate he was about this and how much it meant to him. My job meant a lot to me, sure, but had I ever felt that passion?

When he finished speaking, he smiled at me. "I guess I should tell you about the idea I had that I mentioned in my text. Your friend beat me to it, though."

"What?"

"I was going to suggest that you invite a few colleagues for drinks, somewhere relaxed and neutral, where you can leave easily."

I groaned. Loudly.

There was no getting out of this, was there?

JJ

"What are we doing here? Really?" Niccolò stared around us, his brows raised as he took in the upmarket wine bar we'd just entered. "This isn't our usual kind of place."

Dexter tapped his chin, his lips curving upwards. "I dunno about you, but I'm getting ideas for a scene with a hot businessman in a bar. Working off some tension after a hard day in the office. I'm sure I could re-enact this in the studio."

I rolled my eyes, tugging them both forwards. "Be quiet, both of you, and I'll tell you why we're here. Long story short—I had a one-night thing with a man who turned out to be one of the lecturers at LSU—and no, I didn't know who he was at the time, and he had no idea I was a student. We ran into each other again by accident when I was delivering one of Ander's assignments to him. By the way, Ander doesn't know about any of this, and neither do any of his friends. Please keep it to yourselves."

Nic's eyes were huge as he stared up at me. "Why?" he breathed, completely enraptured. It made me smile.

"Because he's got a reputation for being a bit...uh, harsh. I've heard complaints about him from almost all the business studies students I know. And that leads me to our mission tonight." Pausing for a moment, I debated the best way to phrase my mission without giving away too many details. "I want to see how he acts around his work colleagues outside of a work environment. I want to know if this brusque personality extends to the people he works with or if it's just reserved for his students."

"But why?"

"Because—"

"You fucked again, didn't you?" Dexter interrupted, narrowing his gaze. "It wasn't just a one-night thing."

"So what if I did?"

"You don't fuck people more than once...not unless it's uncomplicated. And from the little you've told us, this sounds to me like the very definition of complicated."

"It's not complicated."

"Then why do you need to see how he acts around his colleagues?"

"Because—because...I'm interested."

Dexter shook his head, patting my arm. "Oh dear. Better start spreading the word. Gay hearts are gonna break all over London when people hear the news that you're off the market."

"Stop that. I'm not off the market. You know that's not me. He would be horrified to hear you say that, too. It's just a bit of fun between us."

Dexter looked unconvinced, but thankfully, he dropped

the subject. My heart skipped a beat, though, because how long had it been since my failed house party blowjob, which was the last time I even tried something with anyone else?

I'd just been busy, that was all.

You never used to be too busy for sex with as many people as possible.

Clenching my jaw, I stomped over to the bar to order a drink. Out of the corner of my eye, I could see Dex and Nic exchanging glances. Fuck. It wasn't like they thought it was. Why had I decided to bring them here? I could've come alone. Or not come at all.

Closing my eyes, I breathed in, then out, calling on my dance training to ground me. When I opened them, I instantly felt more like myself again.

Okay. Back to my usual mode.

"A French 75, please," I purred at the cute bartender. "Dexter, Niccolò? Same?"

Dexter shrugged, and Niccolò gave me two thumbs up. "Make that three, darling."

"Coming right up." The bartender eyed me from beneath his lashes, and we both knew exactly what his sultry look was all about. I was about to make an attempt to return his smile when all my attention was stolen by something across the bar. Some*one.*

My stomach flipped. Looking more gorgeous than he had any right to was Killian. Tonight, he was wearing a deep blue shirt with the sleeves rolled up to his elbows and the top two buttons undone. He'd paired it with black trousers that looked the same as those he wore to work, but with the way he'd lightly tousled his hair, the dark shadow on his jaw, and the casual styling of his shirt, he looked very approachable and very, very dangerous. Dangerous to my sanity because if I didn't get my hands and mouth on him in the next—

"JJ!"

Shiny blue fingernails fluttered in my vision as Nic snapped his fingers in front of me. I blinked, the sounds of the bar filtering back in, and realised that our drinks were ready, and Nic, Dex, and the bartender were all staring at me.

"Sorry." I dug my debit card out of my wallet and tapped it on the card reader, trying not to wince at the price. I should be used to it, especially working in the VIP section of an elite club, and okay, I did have expensive taste in drinks—or so Ander always told me—but even so, three cocktails at this bar were eye-wateringly expensive.

Dexter dipped his head to my ear as we picked up our drinks. "Is he one of the guys across the bar from us?"

"Yeah. Navy shirt. Dark hair. Fucking gorgeous."

"Mmm. I can see why you keep coming back for more." He scanned Killian, his gaze appreciative, and I had a sudden, horrible urge to claw out my friend's eyeballs to stop him from looking at Kill that way.

Swallowing hard, I picked up my drink. My hand was unsteady. What was wrong with me tonight?

Dexter turned to whisper something to Niccolò, and then they were both eyeing my doctor like he was a particularly delicious cocktail. "Oooh. He's lovely," Nic murmured. "Not my type, but *definitely* yours."

"Can you both stop staring at him? I don't want him to know we're here. Remember, we're meant to be discreetly observing him." There would probably be a point when he noticed me, but I wanted to avoid it for as long as possible.

Niccolò's mouth fell open, and he placed his hand on his chest. "I'm discreet!"

"Come on." I dragged them both towards a table that had just become available, still giving me a good view of Killian but nowhere near his line of sight. As my friends fell into conversation, I watched Killian. Gage had joined him in the time we'd been seating ourselves, and I noticed that some of the stiffness had disappeared from Killian's shoulders, although when two women and two men appeared, the stiffness returned. Another much older man joined them soon after, who I recognised as the current head of the faculty, Professor Saunders. I only knew this because after Killian had told me about his desire to become the new head, I'd been curious and looked him up on the uni portal.

Sipping from my cocktail, I watched as Killian greeted the newcomers. He seemed polite enough, although there was no sign of a smile on his face, and as soon as the greetings were over, he lapsed into silence, staring into his glass of wine. I noticed Gage elbow him discreetly, then give Professor Saunders a pointed look, but Killian shook his head.

Fuck. This was worse than I thought.

I had to intervene. Even though I'd told myself I was only here to observe, I couldn't just sit there and watch him throw away a perfectly good socialising opportunity.

Picking up my phone, I sent a quick text. As soon as that was done, I steeled myself for the inevitable and said, "I'm going to talk to him. You two stay here and save our table."

Before my friends had time to question me, I slipped out of my seat and headed towards the door at the far side of the bar, hoping Killian would see my message.

There was a long, wide corridor that led to the outdoor smoking area, and I waited halfway down the corridor, leaning against the wall, glancing down at my phone every now and then, but it remained silent.

Then the doors opened, and my doctor was there.

"Hi." My smile was helpless, butterflies going mad inside me as I took him in. His expression was resigned, but the corners of his lips were curving upwards, just enough to be noticeable, and I felt warm all over.

"What are you doing here?" He stared down at me, and I lost myself in those piercing ice-blue eyes. I needed—

His fingers curled around my wrist for a brief moment before he released me. I fucking trembled at his touch.

"Joshua. I don't know why you're here, and you shouldn't be here in case anyone sees...but it's so good to see you."

"I'm being discreet, I promise. Full disclosure—I came because I wanted to see you in action. To see if the situation was really as dire as your friend was making it out to be."

He laughed humourlessly. "It really is that dire. I've only been here ten minutes, and I want to leave."

I shook my head vehemently. "No. You can do this. Just...just pretend that this is something you really want to be doing. Trick your brain into thinking you're having a good time. Channel someone social. Me, for instance." Lightening the atmosphere, I grinned at him. "This is what I would do if I were the one out there. Now, pay attention." Tapping lightly on the top of my cheekbone, right beneath my lower lashes, I said, "First and most important thing—eye contact. Try to hold eye contact with whoever you're talking to. But don't let your eyes glaze over when you get bored, okay? It's fine to look away. Just try and hold contact as much as you can."

"I guess I can do that," he said grudgingly, folding his arms across his chest. "What else?"

"Ask questions. A lot of people—I'm excluding you—love to talk about themselves. You work with these people, and you have plenty of work-related things in common, even if they're not people you'd choose to hang out with outside of work."

"Do you have that?"

"Do I have what?"

"People on your degree course that you'd avoid outside of your degree subject. People you don't even like. Is that possible?"

Good question. Did I? Yeah, there were people on my course I never really interacted with and had no desire to. But actively disliked, no. I didn't have the energy for that. Oh. Apart from Finn, Ander's football friend who ruined my custom trainers. Just kidding. I didn't even dislike him. He had offered to replace them, after all. It wasn't his fault they were irreplaceable. I sighed. "Of course there are people I wouldn't choose to hang around with, but like I said to you, we have dance-related things in common. For everything else, I have my other friends. I guess after growing up with my grandma and being surrounded by so many different people from all walks of life, I find it easy to start up a conversation with almost anyone."

"Yeah." His voice was soft and bitterly sad. "Guess

that's another thing I can blame on my upbringing. Moving around so much…I never really developed the social skills that others take for granted."

Fuck. *Killian.* He looked so lost. I wanted to wrap my arms around him and protect him from the world and at the same time choose violence towards anyone that made him feel like he wasn't fucking amazing, just the way he was. I needed to tread carefully because the last thing I wanted to do was add to his issues.

I swallowed around the sudden lump in my throat. "You have the skills. And I know that for a fact because I've seen you with G, and she was a complete stranger to you. You're relaxed around Gage, and with me…from the first moment we met—"

"I don't seem to remember us doing much talking." Heat flared in his gaze.

"You knew what you wanted, and you took it. Do the same thing here tonight. Take what you want. You deserve that promotion, Kill. You're fucking amazing at what you do."

He smirked at me then, and just like that, my entire body relaxed, warmth curling low in my belly. "How do you know I'm amazing at what I do? Have you been stalking me, Mr. Everett?"

"You're the stalker in this relation—uh, I mean, out of the two of us, you're the stalker. I simply have amazing powers of deduction." Fuck, I hoped he hadn't noticed the word I'd almost said. Batting my lashes at him, I gave him a bright smile. "You wouldn't have made it as the principal lecturer if you weren't good. And I've heard my housemates and friends complain about you enough to know that you work your students hard and don't tolerate slackers."

"Fair enough. You forgot something, though."

"What's that?"

Moving closer, he leaned into me, his warm breath skating across my ear, making me shiver. "You followed me here tonight. That makes you the stalker."

"Mmm. Maybe I am. Do you have a problem with that?"

He chuckled darkly. "Oh, I have no problem with that. Not at all."

Was it getting hot in here, or was it the insanely attractive man radiating heat from his body, being all sexy and speaking in that husky voice that made me want him to do bad, bad things to me?

"This is a respectable establishment." Breathing far too hard for someone who was as fit as I was, I stepped back, discreetly adjusting the erection that was insisting on attention. Believe me, in the trousers I was wearing, it was noticeable.

Killian's gaze flicked down, his lips parting, and his hand slowly and deliberately went to the obscene, mouthwatering outline of his cock. "Very respectable."

"Okay. I'm going to go outside and cool off. You...do something about that and then go and try my tips. Good luck. Bye," I said breathlessly, backing away, and he laughed.

"Goodbye, Joshua."

FOURTEEN

KILLIAN

After gathering myself, I followed JJ's advice. Fuck, I'd never reacted to anyone the way I did to him. It was troubling, for all the aforementioned reasons. Too young, too happy and effervescent for me. A student. Wrong. But something even worse was happening to me now. My initial attraction to him had been purely sexual, but now, I wanted not only to fuck him; I wanted him. Wanted to have conversations with him. To hold him in my arms. To see him in my flat, curled up on my sofa in those ridiculous socks, completely at home in my space in a way that no one had ever been.

I wanted him in all the ways it was possible to want someone, but I couldn't have him. Trying to tie down someone like JJ was like trying to catch lightning in a bottle. He was too bright and too beautiful for me.

Honestly, even the thought of keeping him came as a shock. I'd always been...if not satisfied with my life, I was indifferent, at the very least, and here he was, stealing my time, turning my ordered world upside down, making me look at things from a completely new point of view. He was so different to anyone else I'd ever known before, so different from me, but somehow, it was so easy between us, and I didn't think either of us understood how or why.

I glanced across the bar, making sure that none of my colleagues noticed. I'd been sneaking looks at him all evening. He drew my attention like nothing and no one else. There he was, standing against the wall, a cocktail in hand, with two other guys who seemed just as confident and self-assured as he was. One was around the same height and build as JJ, with a vaguely familiar face, and the other was a short, twink-ish guy with a mop of dark hair. Together, they made an incredibly good-looking trio, and they spoke to each other with expressive hand gestures and smiles on their faces, at ease and comfortable in each other's presence in the way that only close friends could be.

I envied their ease.

Turning back to Gage, who I'd finally managed to draw into conversation after making the rounds—thanks to JJ's voice in my head—I said, "Are you happy now?"

He smirked at me. "About you being here? I'm fucking ecstatic, mate. Honestly? I thought you wouldn't show up, even though both Stuart and I begged you to." His smirk disappeared, and he stepped closer. "Seriously, thanks for coming. Not that I had anything to do with organising this, but Stuart was saying his wife's had a tough time. She gave up work when they had their kids, and he said she really missed socialisation. Apparently, she gets a year's maternity leave or something, but she's going a bit crazy being at home all day with no adult contact."

"Being at home with no adult contact sounds—actually,

no. I could do without the contact, but not the being at home part. I'm out of the flat at six in the morning most days, and I don't usually return until the evening." Usually late in the evening, thanks to the long hours in my office, and most of the time, when I got home, it wasn't long before I fell into bed after eating. Then in the mornings, I'd wake up at five, get to the gym for six, and have an hour's workout before showering and grabbing coffee on my way to work. My routine had been a little disrupted lately, thanks to JJ's presence, and while it would usually leave me feeling out of control, somehow, I didn't mind when it came to him.

I sighed, and Gage misinterpreted the sound. "Yeah, you work too hard. I'm glad you're finally beginning to realise it."

"That wasn't—"

Gage nudged me in the side with his elbow. "Never mind that. Go on, talk to John. Butter him up a bit. He's the one retiring, but he has an active role in the recruitment process for his successor."

"Fine."

He laughed, nudging me again, and I shot him a glare before resigning myself to the fact that I was going to have to do this if I wanted any peace. And if it meant I could get out of here sooner, even better.

"John. What are you drinking? Can I get you another?"

John glanced up at me, surprise flickering in his gaze. "Killian. Oh. Yes. I'll take another of those..." He squinted towards the bar. "The tap with the blue label. Thank you."

"I'll be right back." Turning to the bar, I ordered him a pint and another glass of Marlborough Sauvignon Blanc for myself. I'd need to make this one last because the last thing I wanted was to end up tipsy around my work colleagues. I had a strict two-drink policy every time I was dragged out to forcibly socialise.

When I returned, John accepted the drink with a word of thanks, and I attempted a smile, JJ's words playing in my mind. Eye contact. Conversation. Work-related. I could do this.

Lightly clasping the stem of my glass, I focused on John's face. "What are your plans for retirement? Will you miss the place, or are you glad to see the back of it?"

Rubbing a hand over his silvery beard, he pursed his lips in thought. "Ah, the question without a true answer. I have several things in the works. The wife has her eye on an Alaskan cruise, so no doubt that'll be first on the agenda. My allotment needs replanting, so that's another, and we're thinking of downsizing, maybe getting a bungalow or even a flat. Something more manageable in the long term." After swigging from his pint, he continued. "I'll miss the place. Been there for years. To be honest, though, I don't think I'll miss the students. Maybe my tolerance has depleted over the years, but they seem so...immature. Young people these days..." He grimaced, and I had to lift a hand to my mouth to hide my own grimace, although mine was for a completely different reason to his.

"Sounds like a good time for you to retire," I said through gritted teeth, following my words with a large gulp of wine.

Lifting his brows, he eyed me with amusement. "I hear you're angling for my job." Thankfully, he didn't seem to expect a response from me. "Play your cards right, and you've got it in the bag. Or should I say—keep playing your cards right. Dependable Dr. Wilder with an incredible work ethic, always going above and beyond, never any hint of a scandal, instilling a healthy respect for authority in impressionable young minds. For what it's worth, you have my vote if things continue as they are."

I coughed, jerking my head once in a movement that I hoped would come off as an agreement. Fuck. This was my reputation, wasn't it? My gaze slid to Stuart, who was watching me with interest, and I attempted to silently communicate that I needed help. Whatever expression he saw on my face had him heading straight over to us, smoothly cutting into the conversation. "Killian, excuse me. Could I have a quick word with John? John, I wondered if we could discuss..."

Their voices faded, becoming indistinguishable among the crowds as they melted away, and I took another large gulp of wine, my mind racing.

My reputation was going to get me my dream job.

I could socialise—tonight had proved it, even if I found it difficult.

I just needed to continue as I was, which meant...

My eyes connected with a pair of bright blue ones all the way over on the other side of the room, and the stab of pain felt almost physical.

It meant that I couldn't afford to continue this...thing—whatever it was—with JJ. The risk was too great.

His eyes widened, and I could see the concern in them, even from the distance of my position from his. But then he broke eye contact as his friend leaned into him, saying something that made JJ smile warmly and the shorter guy grin at them both. They were so different from me.

Tearing my gaze away, I deliberately turned my back, interrupting my colleagues' heated discussion on teaching methods and throwing myself into the conversation. This, I could do.

When I turned around again a little while later, JJ and his friends were nowhere to be seen.

I knew I needed to end this thing between us, but like a fucking addict that had told themselves to quit so many times but didn't have the willpower, I sent him a text.

ME:

Where are you?

JJ:

At my favourite place. I don't have to work tonight, so I'm making the most of it

The text was followed by a photo of a bare, toned torso and long legs encased in the tight fucking trousers I'd done my best not to notice earlier. His bulge was clearly visible, highlighted by a rainbow of coloured lights across his body, his surroundings thrown into shadow.

My dick pulsed, and my jaw clenched as I stabbed out an immediate reply.

ME:

WHERE ARE YOU?

JJ:

Come and find me, baby

Baby. My lip curled. What the fuck. I ignored the way my heart was pounding, about to type out another message when another picture came through. A bar with a cocktail in the foreground. Just behind the cocktail, I could see the torso of the bartender. I zoomed in on the logo on their T-shirt.

I didn't bother replying. Instead, I continued my streak of acting completely irrationally when it came to Joshua James Everett. I made my excuses and left the bar, hopping into one of the black cabs waiting outside.

The cabbie nodded at me. "Where to, mate?"

"Revolve. Soho."

FIFTEEN

JJ

Chike, Shay's model friend, smiled down at me, raising his cocktail glass to knock it against mine. I returned his smile automatically, but my mind was filled with a certain doctor slash soon-to-be professor. It shouldn't be. I shouldn't have sent those cryptic texts. What the fuck was I doing? I had fun, and I moved on. It was easy. No strings. I'd never had any issues before, so why was it happening now?

And I'd tortured myself by sending that text. It wasn't as if he'd come here. Not my doctor, who was allergic to any and all forms of socialisation.

"Not my fucking doctor," I muttered, which had Dex, Nic, Shay, and Chike all staring at me. Maybe I hadn't been as quiet as I thought. Shit.

"Physical!" Shay suddenly screamed as the opening notes of a new song sounded. He threw his hands in the air, and relief flooded my body as everyone followed his lead, downing the rest of their drinks and strutting onto the dance floor. I joined them, although I was on autopilot. We moved to the music, singing...or shouting along with the lyrics, and I did my best to forget everything else other than the here and now.

The music changed to something a little slower and more sultry, and I felt a body pressing up behind me. I'd done this so many times that I didn't even have to think about my moves. I ground my hips back against my dance partner, feeling the hands gripping me and the bulge digging into my ass.

It felt *wrong*.

I closed my eyes, attempting to block everything else out, leaving only the music and the feel of a warm body against mine.

"Move."

My eyes flew open at the low growl to see Killian, a dark, dangerous look on his face, gripping Chike's bicep and forcibly dragging him away from me.

Fucking hell.

"*Move*. He's mine," he ground out, shoving Chike away and then yanking me into him, his hand an iron grip on my waist. I ended up with my back plastered against his front, his breath hot and heavy in my ear, and the vision of Chike's shocked face echoing in my mind.

"Was that your aim, Joshua? You wanted me to come here so I'd see you with someone else? Wanted to drive me fucking crazy, to make me snap?"

I shivered against him, feeling his grip tighten around me, his hard cock insistently pressing against my ass. I couldn't form words, though. My brain was too scrambled. I'd never expected him to come here, and this possessive display—I'd never—

"I've never had anyone be possessive over me before," I gasped, letting my head fall back against his shoulder.

"I find that hard to believe."

A hard roll of his hips and my breath caught in my throat. There were so many "I'd never" moments tonight. I'd never even thought this would be his scene. My text had been aimed at teasing him, but the fact he was now here...

"Killian. Fuck."

"Yeah, *baby*. Fuck. You call me fucking baby, tell me to come and find you, and then I get here and see someone else all over you. What were you doing with that other man?"

"I-I didn't think you'd come. It meant nothing. We were just dancing. Chike's a friend."

"A friend who wants to fuck you. You drive me so fucking crazy," he rasped into my ear. "Tell me why I'm here in this club that I haven't seen the inside of in over two years. Why I'm with you when I shouldn't be. Why I can't fucking stay away from you."

"Yeah?" I spun in his arms, gripping the back of his neck as I met his heavy-lidded gaze, his eyes crackling with electric fire. "Tell me why I can't get you out of my fucking mind. Why I've never had any trouble moving on until you. You've fucked me up."

His smile was sadistic and completely without humour. "Oh, Joshua. Everything you're feeling, I can guarantee that I'm feeling tenfold. I like order in my life. I don't do this. Ever. So tell me. Why the fuck. Am I here?"

I'd run out of words. So I kissed him.

We kissed, and kissed, and kissed. I forgot where we were, forgot that my friends would have questions for me after this blatant display, forgot everything except for the feel of his hard body against mine and his hot mouth dominating me. I was so fucking turned on, but there was something else beneath the sexual tension that seemed to ignite whenever we were in the same place together. Something that burned hotter and deeper, a part of me that had never craved another person in this way before, something that made me want to know everything about this man and to never let him go.

The realisation had me gasping, ripping myself away from Killian. We stared at one another, chests heaving, the music echoing around us while flashes of light alternated between illuminating us and throwing us into shadow. Killian's pupils were wide and dark, but I noticed the same alarm flaring in his gaze.

"Killian."

"I know." He gripped the back of my neck, pulling me back into him and holding me in place as his mouth went to my ear. "It makes no fucking sense to me, either."

"I'm scared," I whispered.

Wrapping his other arm around my waist, he lowered his head to skim his lips over the spot just beneath my ear. "Me too."

"I need...I think I need to get out of here."

Drawing back, he rested his forehead against mine. "Come on. Let's go."

As I lay on my back on his bed, he stripped me down, so fucking slowly, uncovering me inch by inch. When he got to the final layer of my underwear, he looked up at me, and my breath caught in my throat at the intensity of his gaze. His eyes were so beautiful. *He* was so beautiful. I couldn't breathe. Right here, looking at me like I meant something to him, was my dream man, the only one I wanted.

It was almost too much, but I didn't want it to stop.

"You're so beautiful, Joshua," he rasped, echoing my thoughts about him as he trailed his lips up my body, a line of fire following in their wake. "I—" Cutting himself off, he buried his face in my ribcage, his breaths hot and fast against my skin. I stroked my fingers through his hair, completely overcome by feelings I'd never experienced before, drowning under a wave of powerful emotion that stole the breath from my lungs.

He kissed my chest and then up to my collarbone, so softly. His stubble dragged across my skin in the most delicious way, and I shivered beneath him. "Killian," I managed, my voice cracking over his name. He raised his head, his eyes meeting mine, so wide and dark with arousal and something else I couldn't put a name to, but it looked a lot like the way I felt.

I tugged him up to me, and his lips met mine, drinking me in, making me gasp into his mouth. I ran my nails down his back, needing to feel his bare skin against mine, and so I rolled us over so he was lying beneath me, gazing up at me with his lips parted, his chest rising and falling with his panted breaths.

My fingers shook as I worked open the buttons of his shirt, the hard lines of his body coming into view as the material fell open. I stroked across his chest, the light dusting of hair rasping beneath my palm, and felt his pounding heartbeat, strong against my hand.

His hands gripped my thighs. His Adam's apple bobbed as he swallowed hard, his voice so fucking low and wrecked. "JJ. I want you so fucking much."

"Kill. Please. I want you, too."

He helped me get his trousers off because my hands were still shaking—and what the fuck was that all about?—and then all that was between us was our underwear, slick skin sliding together, his body warm and solid against mine. Tugging down his boxer briefs and then mine, he stared down between us at the evidence of our arousal, his fingers curving around my erection. I moaned, his hand the perfect pressure, stroking over my hardness, his calloused thumb rubbing over the tip, smearing my precum around the head.

His gaze flicked to mine, and he licked his lips. "Do you ever top?"

I stared at him. "Um." Clearing my throat, I tried again. "Sometimes, yeah. If I'm in a toppy mood. Do—do you want—"

Cutting off my words with a kiss, he twisted us both so I was beneath him again, the weight of his body pressing mine into the mattress.

"Not tonight, but yes, I want you inside me."

Fuck. "Yeah. Okay. Yes. We can do that."

A smile curved over his lips. "I want you in every way I can have you. You've turned me into an addict, Joshua James. Earlier tonight, I was telling myself that this thing between us needed to end, that you're too young for me, too wrong for me, and we have nothing in common. But now here you are, in my bed, and I'm finding it impossible to let you go."

"It's the same for me," I whispered against his lips,

stroking my hand over the stubble on his jaw and then up the side of his face to slide my fingers through his soft hair. "I can't stop thinking about you, and it scares me so much."

"There are very few things that scare me, but you—this—I'm scared, too," he rasped. "Do you have any idea what you do to me?"

I couldn't reply, so I kissed him. Again and again and again, losing myself in this man who was just as much at a loss as I was, adrift, caught up in feelings that neither of us understood.

He kissed me again, holding me so fucking tightly. "Joshua. Have you...fuck. Have you been tested? Can I fuck you bare? I'm negative for everything, and I just want—"

"Yes," I whispered. "Fucking yes. *Please*. I've been tested recently, and I haven't been with anyone else since..." *Fuck*. I inhaled shakily. "Since I walked into your office for the first time."

His eyes widened, and then his mouth came down on mine, hard and desperate. I wanted him so fucking badly. I wanted him to be mine. I wanted to tell him that there was no one else. That he was the only one for me.

When he pushed inside me after spending what felt like hours opening me up with his fingers, I had to blink back tears. All I could do was hold on, wrapping myself around him as his body moved against mine with slow rolls of his hips, his cock brushing over my prostate every time, sending pleasure curling through my body, my dick and my heart aching at the pure fucking tenderness he was pouring all over me.

When I came, it was a full-body experience, from my head to my toes, goosebumps springing up all over my skin and my heart beating out of my chest. I shook against him, the tears I'd been blinking back spilling over. I sucked in a deep, shuddering breath, pulling Killian's head into the crook of my neck as he filled me with his release.

"My sunshine," he murmured, so quietly that I wasn't sure if I heard him correctly.

I swallowed around the lump in my throat.

I'd always been in control of my life. Always.

Now, I was floundering, and I didn't know what to do.

SIXTEEN

JJ

"What do I do, Sid?" Flopping back on my bed, I rubbed my hands over my face. "This is something I never imagined happening. I caught feelings for him, and I don't know what to do."

In his tank, Sid chewed on a lettuce leaf, his stalk eyes focused on me. It seemed like he was listening, and Ander swore that talking to him was therapeutic. So here I was. Spilling my heart to a snail.

"The odds are stacked against us. We're so different. Neither of us has any experience of relationships, and neither of us even wants to be in one. I'm a student. He's a lecturer at my uni. He thinks we have nothing in common. He thinks I'm young, and yeah, okay, there's an age difference, but my fucking soul knows his. We're connected." My voice dropped to a whisper. "I never meant for any of this to happen, but I don't want to give him up. It would tear me apart."

"Who is he?"

I lowered my hands, my blurry gaze focusing on my

housemate filling the doorway, a frown pulling his brows together, his arms folded across his chest.

No. Not him. Anyone but him. "Ander. What are you doing here?"

"Who is he?" he repeated. Stepping into my bedroom, he took a seat at the end of my bed. "I think I have an idea, but I need to hear you say it."

Fuckfuckfuck.

"You know who it is." When he just stared at me, his mouth in a thin line, I gave up. "It's Dr. Wilder."

Ander collapsed with a loud, pained groan, burying his face in my duvet. He punched my mattress twice, and then he raised his head, an anguished expression on his face. "You couldn't have picked someone else to fall for? Literally *anyone* else?"

"Sorry."

"You have the worst taste, just FYI."

Hot tears stung the backs of my eyelids, but I refused to let them fall. "Thanks."

With a sigh, he pulled himself into a sitting position. "You know how I feel about him."

"Yes, I know," I bit out. To my horror, my voice cracked, and I tore my gaze away, turning away from him so I could hide my face.

"JJ." Ander's fingers landed on my arm, and he tentatively patted it. "Sorry. I didn't...fuck. I'm sorry. It's... fucking hell, bro, I don't know what to say."

I remained silent, and he sighed again. The bed dipped, and then his breath was hitting my ear. "JJ, I really am sorry. I didn't know he was important to you. You never...you're like me. You don't catch feelings."

"You changed, and I guess I'm changing, too."

His hand moved from my arm, curling around my waist in a slow, hesitant movement. "This is so fucking weird," he muttered under his breath, but he held on to me, and after a moment, I allowed myself to relax against him. Eventually, he broke the silence with yet another sigh. "I guess I'm gonna have to try really hard in his class now."

I sniffed, trying to compose myself. This wasn't like me. Adrift, unsure, overwhelmed with feelings I couldn't parse through. "I don't know how it happened, but it did, and I... he's... It's not going to go away."

"Yeah. You know I'm shit with advice. Sid's probably better than me. But for what it's worth, if the way you feel about him is even a little bit like the way I feel about Elliot, don't let him go."

"There's no future for us." In the weirdest turn of events ever between me and my housemate, I turned around, buried my face in his shoulder, and finally let my tears fall. He held me silently and let me cry.

Much later, I lifted my head, rubbing at my swollen eyes. "Sorry."

Ander released his grip on me, rolling to his back with a huff of laughter. "Don't be sorry. You know I'm here for you, always." He cleared his throat. "Not gonna lie, that was a bit weird. Nothing to do with you, just me...y'know. I'm not the person who comforts other people. Not unless it's Elliot, anyway."

"You're better at it than you think." I already felt lighter. "I appreciate you. And Sid."

"Yeah. Sid's great." He shot a grin in the direction of the snail. "So. Uh. Now that's over. Want to work on a plan?"

"A plan?"

"Yeah. When I was eavesdropping, I heard you say he thinks you have nothing in common. You want to change his mind, right?"

Did I?

Fuck. Whatever my brain told me, I knew it wasn't that easy. I wanted Killian. Even if it didn't make any sense. Even if I didn't want a relationship.

"What do you suggest?"

"Simple." Ander turned the full force of his bright white grin on me. "You teach. He teaches. Take him to your dance group, and he can see the evidence that you're both teachers."

"My dance group?" I taught a weekly dance class at a local youth centre, which I'd been involved in since September when one of my lecturers had suggested it as a way to gain experience. I wanted to be a choreographer eventually, and teaching teenagers to dance gave me solid experience for the future, and I loved it.

A reluctant smile spread across my face.

"My dance group," I repeated, watching as Ander gave me an encouraging nod. Out of the corner of my eye, there was a slow, fluid movement from the tank, and for a second, I could almost delude myself into thinking that Sid was giving me a nod of approval, too.

SEVENTEEN

KILLIAN

Horizons Youth Centre. I glanced up at the sign before shaking my head and pushing open the door. I had no idea why JJ had insisted on my being here, but I'd been intrigued when I received his text. All he'd said was that there was something we had in common, and then he'd added a time and the address of this place.

"Can I help you?"

I stopped dead inside the doors. A man with salt-and-pepper hair and a kind, weathered face was standing in front of me, a mug of something steaming hot in one hand and a large binder in the other.

"I'm looking for JJ."

A smile spread across his face. "Of course. You must be Killian. I'm Nick, director of the youth centre. JJ's just down the hall. Go all the way to the end, turn left, and then it's the second door on the right."

He knew who I was? "Thanks," I managed, attempting to return his smile, although it felt false.

"Don't mention it." He stepped aside to let me pass.

Straightening my shoulders, I followed his directions, ending up in front of a nondescript door. When I pushed it open, the first thing I saw was a mirrored wall directly in front of me, reflecting my apprehensive expression.

The second thing I noticed was JJ, clad in black dance tights and a loose, royal blue sleeveless exercise top. His cheeks were flushed, and his hair was damp, sticking out in every direction. A small group of teenagers that looked to be somewhere between thirteen and sixteen surrounded him, clamouring for his attention. His eyes were alight with humour as he responded to them, and something inside me warmed. This time, my smile came easily.

Clapping his hands together, he addressed the group. "Alright! Let's run through it from the beginning." Shortly afterwards, music sounded from the speakers, and the group began to dance. I watched, mesmerised. They were completely in sync, concentration on their faces as they moved, swept up in the music. JJ was caught up in the dance, completely focused on his students and occasionally calling out instructions, and as I watched, I realised why he'd wanted me to see this.

My sunshine boy was a teacher, like I was. He had students who wanted to learn from him.

And he was very, very good at what he did.

When he noticed me, a wide smile curved over his lips, although he tried to bite it back. His attention was quickly stolen by his students, though, and I rested against the cool breeze blocks that made up the side wall, my arms folded across my chest, watching him work. He seemed to have endless patience and words of encouragement for everyone.

The opposite of the way I taught. Perhaps he'd been

right. I was a teacher, but I still needed to learn. I couldn't adopt his teaching style—it was almost the antithesis of mine—but maybe I could attempt a more encouraging method with my students.

Maybe.

The class eventually came to an end, the teenagers trailing out of the door in a slow trickle, most stopping to speak to JJ before they left. I noticed that every single one of them had a smile on their faces.

Finally, we were alone. I stepped into the centre of the room, catching JJ around the wrist as he walked past me in the direction of the dock where he'd placed his phone.

"Not so fast," I murmured, pulling him into me. Before he could respond, I gripped his throat and lowered my head, my mouth meeting his.

He melted against me, wrapping his arms around my shoulders, his tongue sliding against mine as he deepened the kiss. When we broke apart, he gave me a soft smile.

"Hello, Dr. Wilder. What did you think of my dance class?"

"You were amazing," I said truthfully.

A flush bloomed on his cheeks, and I had to kiss him again. This time, when we drew apart, both of us were breathing heavily, and my dick was tenting my trousers. With his parted lips glistening from our kisses, he stared at me with darkened eyes, so fucking gorgeous, flushed and aroused.

I took a step back from him, for my own sanity as well as his. I couldn't let us get carried away, not here. Rubbing my hand over my jaw, I cleared my throat. "Show me your dance."

"My dance?"

"Mmm. The one you're working on for your showcase."

His eyes flew to mine, widening. "My individual one?"

"Yes." He'd spoken at length about it to me, and I'd found myself invested in his passion and fire, and, well, if I were honest with myself, I wanted to know everything that was important to him.

The surprise melted away, replaced with that sexy confidence he had in spades. "Go and sit over there." He pointed towards the single row of chairs on either side of the door. "I haven't finished choreographing it yet, but I'll give you a preview of the part of it I've been working on this week." By the time I'd taken a seat, he was in position, poised, ready for the song to begin.

The first notes sounded, and he *moved.*

Moved like no one else I'd ever seen before. I'd seen him dancing with Alyssa and Leo, I'd seen him dancing on a pole, I'd had an up close and personal view of him dancing on me, and I'd been blown away each and every time. But this...this was another level. This man in front of me was so fucking talented it took my breath away.

I watched, completely captivated, unable to tear my eyes from him until the dance finished. When he came to a stop, his chest rising and falling rapidly, I rose to my feet and strode towards him, capturing his lips with mine.

"Come home with me."

He shook his head. "I can't. I've got a shift at Sanctuary tonight."

"And you have uni tomorrow morning?"

"Yeah. That's where my sweet, sweet coffee comes in handy."

Irrational anger burned inside me. "You need to slow down. Take care of yourself."

Another shake of his head. "No, I don't. I'm fine, Killian. I'm not taking on more than I can handle. You have to trust me."

My jaw clenched as I stared at him. I didn't like this. I knew he took on a lot, what with his degree, working at Sanctuary, and his commitment to his grandma, not to mention his social life. It already seemed like a huge load for him to bear, and I hadn't even known about this dance class until today.

"Don't give me that look. Please. I'm fine, I promise. If it was too much, I'd slow down."

"I don't like the thought of you taking on too much," I muttered, pulling him into my arms.

He sighed against me. "You're one to talk, with your staying late at work and forgetting to eat. What about a compromise? You can come to the club. Stay for a bit—not the whole night, because you need your sleep. See that I'm coping just fine."

Go to a nightclub on a weeknight when I had a full day of lectures the following day?

It should have been an easy no, but instead, I found myself saying yes.

EIGHTEEN

KILLIAN

"Killian Wilder. Principal business lecturer at London Southwark University."

My gaze flew from the whisky glass gathering condensation on the booth table to the suited man who stood in front of me, studying me intently. Tall, dark-haired, green-eyed, probably mid-twenties, extremely good-looking —but not even close to my type—he scrutinised me just as closely, one brow raised.

"Sorry, who are you?"

He held out his hand. "Austin De Witt. JJ's boss."

Austin De Witt. Gage had told me about him—it was thanks to his old school connection with Austin that we'd been admitted to the VIP area that first night when I'd met JJ. He was part owner and the manager of Sanctuary, and he worked closely with a man named Credence Pope, whom I knew from the grapevine was a very powerful man with connections that most people could only dream of.

In short, Austin De Witt was someone you didn't want to get on the wrong side of.

Clearing my throat, I shook his hand briskly. "Good to meet you."

"JJ's one of my most popular members of staff," he said. "Bear that in mind."

Then he turned on his heel and strode away, shoving his hands in his pockets in a display that screamed of casual power. This was a man who was used to being in charge. A man who wouldn't hesitate to fuck someone over if they wronged him. I knew that in my bones.

Strangely, it helped me relax a little. If JJ had someone like that looking out for him, I knew he wouldn't come to any harm or overwork himself while he was here.

A spotlight clicked on over the pole my booth was facing, and I sat forwards, both Austin and my whisky forgotten. When the first notes sounded and I realised it was the same song that had been played in JJ's dance class, my jaw dropped.

But this was *nothing* like his dance class.

This was one hundred percent. Pure. Fucking. Sex.

JJ was dressed in silver booty shorts and nothing else, writhing on the pole, his toned, oiled, glittering body curving around the metal cylinder like it was an extension of him. My mouth was dry, and my heart was pounding so hard I felt lightheaded.

Fucking hell.

This man.

Twenty fucking years old, and he made my cock as hard as stone and my heart race like no one else ever had before.

Twenty years old. A student at the university I taught at. Someone I should never have even seen in a sexual way, and yet I had, and from the first moment I'd seen him, I'd wanted him so badly.

And oh, how I wanted him still.

He curved one of his calves around the pole, hanging upside down, and then straightened his legs, sliding down the pole. So fucking sexy. I prided myself on my control, but right then, I felt like I was going to come in my fucking pants like a teenager just from watching him. He was better than any porn, turned me on more than anyone or anything I'd seen in my life.

"What am I supposed to do?" I whispered, my words hidden by the sultry beat of the music he was dancing to.

There was no answer.

***

"Austin's gone home. No one will know." JJ tugged me through the door that led to the staff areas, the door I wasn't supposed to go through. As usual, my brain was scrambled around him, and I allowed myself to be led into the off-limits area. JJ glanced back at me, his eyes sparkling, the blues popping against the shimmering black liner.

"Kill. Don't worry. I wouldn't bring you back here if there was an issue."

My brows rose against my will, and JJ shook his head, huffing out a breath.

"As I said, Austin's gone home, and no one else will disturb us. It's okay." He made a point of locking the door behind us, although the reassurance of the lock was somewhat negated by the fact that the door could be opened from the other side via a keypad. I'd noticed one of the other dancers giving us a knowing look as we'd passed her, and the thought was enough to send a rush of jealousy through my veins.

"Have you brought anyone else back here? That first night, you told me you'd never fucked anyone at work before. Is that still true?"

He glanced back at me as he led me into the same changing area we'd been in on our first night. "Why? Jealous?"

"Joshua," I growled, pressing up against his back, my fingers curving around his throat. His pulse was rapid beneath my grip. Pressing my mouth to his shoulder, I bit down, and he shuddered.

"Fucking hell, Killian. Where's all this possessiveness coming from?"

"Answer the fucking question."

"No. There's been no one else back here. You're the only one."

I placed a soft, open-mouthed kiss to the place I'd bitten, and he laughed against me, low and warm. "Happy now, my jealous lover?"

"Jealous lover," I muttered under my breath, wrapping my other arm around his waist. Continuing to press kisses along his shoulder, I stroked across the lines of his abs, feeling them contracting beneath my fingertips. Time to change the subject. "Last time we were in here, you said something about being able to suck your own dick." Lowering my hand, I rubbed my palm over the growing bulge in his shorts, making his breath hitch as his head rolled back against my shoulder.

"You want a demonstration, do you?" Stepping out of

his shorts, letting his hard cock spring free, he gracefully lowered himself to the bench seat, his legs slightly spread, and gave me a sultry look from beneath his lashes.

"Fuck, yes. Do it."

He gripped the underside of his thighs, lifting them slowly, then just rolled his body over, his mouth meeting the tip of his cock.

My jaw dropped. Yes, I knew he was extremely flexible, but seeing this...his mouth closing over the head of his cock and *sucking*...

His tongue swirled around the head as he lifted his gaze to mine again, and I groaned low in my throat.

Releasing his grip on his thighs, he grasped the base of his cock and then raised his head. A smirk tugged at his lips. "As you can see, I can suck my own dick. But I'd much rather suck yours."

"*Yes.*" My hands made quick work of my trousers, and when I released my aching cock, I stepped up in front of him, taking hold of his jaw. "Suck."

"Fuck my mouth. Don't hold back," he murmured, and my dick jerked. His lashes fluttered as he leaned forwards, encompassing my dick in the wet heat of his mouth. I moaned, thrusting forwards, and he gripped the backs of my thighs, tugging me even closer, taking my erection all the way to the base. Tears filled his beautiful eyes as he let me fuck his throat, losing all semblance of control. One of his hands dropped from my thigh, and through the haze of pure fucking pleasure, I was dimly aware that he was working over his own cock faster and harder, moaning around my length as we both chased our release.

"Coming..." I panted, my body curling over as I shot

down his throat, feeling his throat contracting around my pulsing cock. Seconds later, a warm wetness hit my thigh, and his head jerked backwards and thudded against the wall, JJ gasping for breath, overcome by his own release.

Neither of us spoke as we cleaned up. We were both way out of our depth, unexpected feelings lying heavy and unspoken between us.

The silence was broken by JJ's soft gasp. "It's three o'clock. My shift's over now."

Three in the morning? How had I lost track of time? I was normally up at five on a weekday to go to the gym by six.

"Well, I guess that's my cue to go home." My voice came out hoarse. I didn't want to leave him, but I needed to. Yet I found myself saying, "You can come with me if you want to. To sleep. We can get the Tube together tomorrow."

His wide-eyed gaze flew to mine. "You want me to come back to your flat. To sleep."

I licked my lips and then cleared my throat. "Yes."

A soft smile curled his lips upwards. "Okay. I'll come."

NINETEEN

JJ

That moment in the early hours of the morning, when the sky is just beginning to lighten and everything feels a little unreal...that's when it's easiest to bare your soul.

Lying in Killian's bed, his curtains partially open to let in the dawn, his arm wrapped securely around me as I laid my head on his shoulder, I shared more details of my life growing up with G and my dreams of becoming a choreographer. When I'd finished talking, we lay in silence for a while, my fingers stroking across his chest, playing with the light smattering of hairs there, until he sighed.

"I want to share with you, too. I... It's hard. Growing up, I was shunted from one foster home to the next. My birth parents were...well, I never knew them. Prison, drugs...they had no interest in me and no capability for looking after me. I never really experienced love. It always felt like my foster families were taking me in under a sense of obligation. Perhaps that was me projecting, but it was the way I always felt."

My heart *hurt*. So, so much. This beautiful, lonely man,

who had so much to give, had never known unconditional love. Had felt unwanted and rejected.

I blinked rapidly, desperately trying to hold back my tears, because I sensed that if he saw how upset I was, he'd stop talking, and I wanted him to continue. I wanted to know everything about him. I wanted him to share everything with me. I wanted to be the person who he confided in. The person who could show him the love he'd never had.

Wait.

Love.

Was that what I felt for Killian?

It was too big to comprehend. I locked it away and concentrated on him. Only him. My wonderful, complicated doctor.

"The final straw came when I was seventeen, and my foster mother accused me of stealing her rent money. I hadn't touched it, but...suffice to say, she didn't believe me. She got my foster dad involved, and after the beating he gave me, I packed my rucksack with everything I had, and I left. I...it was a struggle for a while, but I had plenty of incentive to succeed, and that was what I did." His voice grew stronger. "I got perfect results in my A levels and was instantly accepted to a business degree course. I've been throwing myself into work ever since. Always trying to better myself. To prove that I mean something. That—" He paused, sucking in a shocked breath, as if something had just occurred to him. "*That's* why I want this promotion," he continued, his voice full of wonder. "So I can prove that I mean something."

Oh, fuck.

There was no way I could stop my tears, not now, and so I buried my face in his pillow, hoping I could hide them from him. He didn't say anything, but I felt him take a few shuddering breaths, so maybe he was struggling just as much as I was.

I didn't trust myself to speak, but I wanted to tell him that he *did* mean something. That he was already so accomplished, and he had nothing to prove to anyone. He meant something to so many people. He'd touched the lives of hundreds of students, even if they didn't all appreciate his teaching methods. He was caring and intelligent and so fucking sexy, and I was the luckiest man in the entire world to have him in my life.

"I-I wish you could see yourself the way I see you," I eventually managed, my voice cracking over the words. "You're amazing, Killian. You don't need to change anything about you. Not one single thing. You have nothing to prove to anyone."

"What the fuck would you know?" His words lashed at me, harsh and unforgiving. I shrank away from him, trying to remind myself that he was feeling vulnerable and raw.

The next second, he was on me, wrapping me in his arms and burying his face in my throat.

"I'm sorry, baby. So sorry. I didn't mean...fuck. I'm sorry."

Twisting in his arms, I met his distraught gaze. "I know you didn't, but please don't take it out on me."

"I know. I'm sorry. You're so...you're— Fuck, JJ. I don't even know what you're doing here with me."

This man. "I'm here because I want to be, okay? Just trust me. I don't do anything I don't want to."

Shaking his head, he pulled me even closer. "My sunshine. I know you're only temporary, but I'll never forget how you lit up my life. How you made everything better."

"Kill—"

Pressing a finger to my lips, he stopped me in my tracks. "Don't speak."

I looked at him, really looked at him, and in the soft light of dawn, I saw the dampness coating his lashes and the sadness in his eyes. I closed my mouth, closed my eyes, and held him.

There was nothing else I could do.

TWENTY

JJ

Ander had been onto something with the dance class, and the way Killian had opened up to me afterwards had been an incredible privilege that I'd never, ever take for granted. He'd been quiet since, or more so than normal, and I'd given him his space because I had the feeling that opening up to me had shaken him. A lot. It had shaken me, too, to be the one he confided in when we were only... whatever we were...in a situationship, maybe, and he kept reiterating that it was temporary and I was too young, and all the other excuses he kept telling us both.

I still wasn't sure what I wanted, either, and I'd been completely unprepared for the way he'd worked his way into my life and made himself at home so easily—despite what he said—but what I did know was that I wanted him to stay, in whatever capacity I could have him. It had been the sex and instant physical attraction that had brought us together, but now it was more. Much more. He was someone I was beginning to care deeply about, and I wasn't going to let him go without a fight. And so, here we were. Ander's dance class idea had, in turn, given me an idea.

"G, you remember Killian, right?"

My grandma rolled her eyes at me and smacked my arm with the magazine she'd been reading. "Yes, Josh, of course I remember your hot doctor." She glanced at Killian, her eyes twinkling merrily, and I steeled myself for whatever was about to come out of her mouth. "He's been the talk of the complex. Very handsome. You make a wonderful couple. I'm so happy I got to see you with your true love before I pass on to higher places."

For fuck's sake. "G. *Please*. Have you been on the gin already?"

Killian's cheeks were flushed, but there was an amused smirk on his face. "Glynis. It's lovely to see you again." Handing her the tiny but ridiculously expensive box of chocolates he'd brought with him, he gave her a genuine smile, taking her free hand and placing a kiss to the back of it. Something inside me fucking *melted*.

"You too, dear." Her gaze flicked back to me. "Josh, I hope you're noting this behaviour down. Your doctor has wonderful manners."

"He does," I said, far too softly and fondly, and both of them stared at me. Clearing my throat, I attempted to regain my usual composure. "I thought he could watch our dance class today."

"Watch? Oh no, my dear. Killian simply must participate." Climbing to her feet, she began muttering to herself while I gritted my teeth, hoping I hadn't made a mistake in bringing Killian back here. "I cannot allow him to dance with Barbara, though. She'll never let me hear the end of it. No, we must practise now so we can show that ho who the most talented dancer is. Oh, yes. This will be fabulous. A throwback to my glory days."

There was a knock on her door, and I strode across the room to open it, leaving Killian to fend for himself.

"JJ!" I staggered backwards as Niccolò threw himself at me.

"Nic? What are you doing here?" Disentangling myself from my friend, I was suddenly aware that it had gone quiet behind me.

"I'm here for the dance class." He peered into the room, his bright smile disappearing, replaced by a frown. "I didn't get the date wrong, did I?"

Fuck. How had I managed to forget that I'd asked Nic to help out? He came with me to the complex as often as he could, having been a frequent visitor at our house growing up, and G adored him.

Rubbing my hand across my face, I shook my head. "No. Sorry, babe. Yeah. The dance class." I stepped aside so he could enter, and my gaze darted to Killian's. His eyes had darkened, his jaw set as he stared daggers at Niccolò.

"Niccolò, darling." G swept him into a hug, and he kissed both of her cheeks, his bright smile returning. "Beware of Kitty—she'll try to monopolise all your attention again."

He laughed. "Don't worry about me, G. I can handle her." Releasing my grandma, he looked back at me, his brows lifting. "JJ? Are you going to introduce me to your friend?"

As if he didn't know who Killian was. "Yeah. Uh, Nic,

meet Killian. Killian, this is Niccolò. One of my best friends."

"Killian's a *doctor*," G interjected, fanning herself. "And he's helping out with our dance class today. We were just about to practise."

"Ooh!" Niccolò clapped his hands together, bounding over to G's armchair. He draped his body over the furniture with an exaggerated sigh, kicking one leg over the other. "Go ahead. I want to see."

"I think Killian and Josh should dance to begin with, don't you, my darling Niccolò?" G took a seat in the other armchair, daintily crossing her ankles.

"You're so right. We should *definitely* watch JJ dance with Killian." Nic smirked at me, and I had a sudden urge to commit violence against my usually sweet friend. He was clearly in cahoots with my grandma, the little traitor.

"Fine," I growled, stalking over to G's record player. The best way to deal with this was to go along with what they wanted and not make a big deal out of it. It wasn't a big deal, anyway. It was just me, dancing with the gorgeous older man I was really into, while two of the people who knew me best scrutinised my every move... Fuck. Who was I kidding? This was going to be a disaster.

Glancing down at the record already on the turntable, I noticed it was the compilation of slow dance songs I'd gifted G for her eighty-first birthday. If I didn't know better, I'd think G had planned this. Wait a minute. She probably *had* planned this.

I lowered the needle to the vinyl, and the opening notes of "Lover" by Taylor Swift sounded. Standing in the centre of the room, where there was space to dance, I lifted my hands, placing one around Killian's and the other at his shoulder. He placed his free hand on my waist, his thumb lightly caressing my side.

Our eyes met, and beneath that storminess that had appeared when Niccolò had shown up, there was something else. Something soft and warm that gave me butterflies and made me melt into him as we began to move to the music.

We danced like we'd been dancing together for years. Killian spun me around the room, his gaze fixed on mine, so elegant and graceful that I almost felt as if we were in a dream.

When the song came to an end, he pulled me into his arms, lowering his head so his lips brushed against my ear. "You're mine. Don't forget it."

With those parting words, he released me, striding across the room to my grandma, where he dropped into a bow. Where the fuck was all this coming from? The dancing, the bowing, the declaration that I was his?

"Glynis. May I have this dance?"

She took his hand, and when the next song began, I choked up, blinking rapidly to keep my composure, because it was an Emily Watts cover of Édith Piaf's "La Vie en rose," G's favourite song ever and one we'd danced to over the years growing up. I was thrown back into memories, spinning around our kitchen as the delicious smells of breakfast cooking wafted around us, the sash windows open to let in the morning breeze, the sounds of a house full of friends slowly waking up, ready to enjoy a lazy Sunday morning.

Arms wound around my waist, and I looked down to see

Nic staring up at me. "This song brings back so many happy memories."

I nodded, unable to speak, my gaze going back to Killian holding G like she was something precious, gently moving her around the floor, murmuring something to her that made her smile widely.

"Oh, fuck. I am in so much trouble," I whispered shakily.

Niccolò's arms tightened around me. "Yeah. You are."

The dance class had finished, and Niccolò had slipped away, leaving me with G and Killian. They were deep in conversation, G sharing one of her tall tales, and I ached. There had been no part of me that had been interested in a relationship until Killian had come into my life, and now I had no idea how I was supposed to let him go.

When we eventually said our goodbyes and were out on the streets, this part of London quiet in the evening, Killian stopped me with a hand to my arm. "Is everything okay? You haven't said much today."

"Yeah." My voice cracked, and I tried again, clearing my throat first. "Yeah. Where did you learn to dance?" I asked because it was the easiest thing to focus on, because I didn't have the words to articulate everything I was feeling inside.

He gave me a bittersweet smile. "It wasn't something I consciously planned. You know I told you I was on my own from seventeen?" When I nodded, he continued. "There was a centre close to me. A little like your youth centre, now I think about it. They had what they called 'outreach' programmes. I attended a few of them. On Tuesdays from six until seven, they ran a dance class, followed by a meal. It was run by volunteers, and we could pay whatever we could afford to attend. Even if someone had no money, they were never turned away. I knew that every Tuesday, if I attended the dance class, I'd get a guaranteed hot meal. It was the same on Thursdays, but that class was teaching business skills. I'm sure it had a hand in my impeccable A-level results."

I almost smiled at his use of the word "impeccable," but I was still stuck on the revelation that he'd attended dance classes in order to get a guaranteed hot meal.

"Is the youth centre still open?"

His lips turned down, and he shook his head. "Unfortunately, they couldn't sustain the funding they needed, and they had to close down. I'll never forget them, though."

Stepping closer to him, I slid my arms around him, leaning my head against his shoulder. I didn't even know what to say in response to his words, and I had a very strong feeling that he'd react badly if I showed him sympathy, so instead, I said, "It's hard. The youth centre I teach at always has funding issues, too. I give what I can, but their overheads are so high. I guess they're lucky that they have generous donors backing them."

He sighed, his arms wrapping around me, tugging me into him so we were holding each other close. I felt a soft kiss on my temple, and then his voice was murmuring in my ear. "Thank you for inviting me today. And to your dance class at the youth centre."

"You're always welcome, Kill. Always. No matter what."

After a deep, shuddering breath, he loosened his grip on me. "Do you want to get some food somewhere?"

I smiled against him. "That sounds nice. Where do you want to go?"

"Wherever we can get a table with no notice. Let's walk."

TWENTY-ONE

KILLIAN

Seated in the tiny, crowded Italian pizzeria, our knees knocking together with the lack of space, I perused the menu as JJ perused me. I could feel his scrutinising gaze, and I knew he probably had questions, one of which most likely involved my irrational jealousy when his friend had shown up earlier.

When the waiter came over and JJ made no move to order, I rattled off a quick list of starters and sides, two pizzas to split, a carafe of wine, and a jug of water. He remained silent, and I slid my hand across the table, covering his.

"JJ. Talk to me."

He blinked a few times, and then he shook his head. "Sorry. It's been... What are we doing here?" His voice lowered. "Why did you tell me I was yours earlier?"

How was I supposed to answer either of those questions when I didn't have a straightforward answer? I had to try, though. I knew he appreciated my being upfront, as did I.

"We're here because I wanted to spend time with you. As for earlier..." Was I really going to have to attempt to put my thoughts into words when I could barely articulate them in my brain? "I'm...I suppose I was a little jealous of how familiar you were with your friend and how well suited you are. G, too. I suppose...I felt a little left out."

JJ growled under his breath, and then he pushed his seat back from the table. Shooting to his feet, he stalked around the table and grabbed hold of my wrist, yanking me out of my seat, and dragged me outside, completely ignoring several shocked whispers that sounded in our wake.

"Listen to me, and listen properly, because I'm only going to say this once. Your jealousy, which, yeah, is fucking hot, is completely misplaced. Nic is my friend. That's it. And yeah, he knows G well because we've grown up together. We went to the same school, and he was a year below me, and I looked out for him. We stuck together. But none of that means you were left out. I don't want Nic. He doesn't want me. G fucking loves you—you've got her wrapped around your little finger already. Fucking hell, Kill, if you could've seen yourself dancing today. It—" He broke off, rubbing at his eyes. "It meant a lot to me to see you with G. You're so good with her. Why can't you see how good you are with her? Why don't you realise that when you're in a room with me, you're all I see?"

My jaw dropped. People passed us, knocking into my side, but I barely noticed. "I'm all you see?"

His bright blue eyes blazed with fire as he stared at me defiantly. "Yes, Dr. Fucking. Wilder. Don't tell me you haven't noticed that."

"Come here," I murmured, gripping the back of his neck and kissing him with everything I had.

When I'd thoroughly subdued him, I held him tightly, trailing kisses over his face, enjoying the way he sighed against me.

"Want to go back inside now?"

He nodded, a small, wry smile tugging at his lips. "Sorry. I didn't mean to get angry with you. You have to know how I— Fuck. Situationships are harder than I thought," he muttered, ducking under my arm to wrap his fingers around the restaurant door handle.

I pulled him backwards, his spine hitting my chest. "Situationships?"

"I think that's the best way of describing this, don't you?" Pulling away from me, he re-entered the restaurant.

In our absence, our water, wine, and a basket of bread had been placed on the table, along with olive oil and balsamic vinegar for dipping. I poured us both some water and wine before offering JJ the bread. "Not really. Not when I don't know what it means."

"Kill. What do you want from me?"

How could I answer that? "Can we just take each day as it comes?"

His shoulders slumped, his whole body losing its tension. "Take each day as it comes. Yes. Let's do that."

Somehow, after that, it was easy. We talked about anything and everything, sharing our food, the restaurant gradually emptying out around us until there were only a couple of other tables of people remaining. I felt a little ridiculous for my reactions earlier. It had been an emotional day—fuck, this entire thing between us had brought things to the surface I'd had no trouble suppressing before, and JJ was clearly as out of his depth as I was. He'd said as much.

At least we were in this together.

Leaving the restaurant, I glanced over at JJ to find him already looking at me. He smiled his sunshine smile, and I knew right then that I'd do anything to keep him smiling at me like that.

"Want to walk for a bit?" I suggested. He nodded, and I wrapped my arm around him, pulling him close. His arm slid around my waist, the smile still playing over his lips, and as we meandered through the quiet streets, wrapped up in each other, I wished we could stay in this moment forever.

I'd been relaxed after the shower followed by the long bath we'd taken together, but now I was stretched out on the bed on my stomach, and JJ's hands were kneading my muscles, turning me boneless, I'd fallen into a dreamlike state. His palms stroked across my glutes, gently pushing them apart as he lowered his body, kissing down my spine.

"Can I rim you?" he murmured into my skin, circling my hole with the tip of his finger. I knew where he was going with this, and I wanted it. Wanted to know how he felt inside me.

"Yes." Burying my face in my pillow, I widened my legs even further, allowing him to settle between them. This position felt so vulnerable to me, and I didn't want to tell him that I'd never let anyone else do this before. I'd never felt this comfortable with anyone. Not until him.

I felt his warm, wet tongue dragging across my sensitive skin, and I moaned at the completely new sensation.

His head rose. "Okay?"

"Mmm."

Another swirl of his tongue, and then another, and another. By the time he slid two fingers inside me, brushing over my prostate, I was rutting back against him, my dick leaking precum over the sheets beneath me, and I was so fucking ready to feel his cock in me.

He curled his body over mine, pressing a kiss to my shoulder. "You like that, Dr. Wilder?"

"Mmm...fuck, Joshua. Need your cock."

"Just a bit longer. I don't want to hurt you." Slowly easing another lubed finger inside me, he opened me up, and then I felt the head of his cock at my hole.

Breathing out as he eased inside, I focused on the sensation of him filling me. He'd done such a thorough job of preparing me that there wasn't even a hint of pain, just fullness as he slid all the way home.

"I think I've died and gone to heaven," he murmured into the back of my neck. "You feel indescribably divine."

I laughed low in my throat. "Does that make me a god?"

"A sex god." He rolled his hips forwards, and we both groaned. "Fuck, Killian."

"Yeah, baby. Keep doing that."

He obliged, the two of us falling into a slow, steady, rolling movement, and it was so different to anything I'd ever experienced before. For a start, I generally preferred to top, so this was a rare experience, but the emotions spilling over between us...I'd never, ever slept with anyone and had an emotional connection with them before him.

When I came, completely untouched and completely overwhelmed, the question was still burning in my mind.

What was it about JJ that made everything so different?

TWENTY-TWO

KILLIAN

"Fuck. That's it." I thrust forwards, my balls tightening up as my dick pulsed, and three things happened at once.

My office door flew open, revealing the shocked face of Gage, a screech tearing from his throat.

JJ fell backwards, knocking his head against the edge of my desk with a pained cry.

Too close to the edge, I couldn't stop my orgasm, and instead of coming down JJ's throat, my cum landed on the floor, the desk, and JJ.

"Get out!" I roared, and the door slammed shut, thankfully with Gage on the other side. Uncaring of my ruined orgasm and the fact that I was now going to be cleaning up cum from my office, I dropped to my knees in front of JJ. He was holding the back of his head, trying to blink back tears, and the only thing I cared about right then was making sure he was okay.

"Hey. Let me see." Gently, I tipped his head forwards,

carefully feeling around. He hissed as I came into contact with a burgeoning lump. "You're hurt."

"It's my fault. I thought I locked the door."

"It's not your fault. It was an accident." If anything, it was my fault. The lock could be temperamental, and I should have double-checked it, but I'd been too distracted with getting my dick in JJ's tempting mouth. Becoming aware of the mess surrounding us, I groaned. "Fuck. Wait just a second." Grabbing a handful of tissues from my desk drawer, I quickly cleaned us as best I could, tugging my trousers up and zipping them shut. Then, I guided JJ into my office chair. "Wait here a minute. I'll be back as quickly as I can, okay?"

A single tear ran down his cheek, and he impatiently swiped it away. "I don't even know why I'm crying."

My jaw clenched, and my stomach hurt. Cupping his chin, I kissed the tear track. His eyes fluttered shut, and I placed a soft kiss to his eyelids before climbing back to my feet. "I'll be back in a minute."

Jogging down the stairs to the staff canteen, I burst through the doors. "I need ice," I barked to the shocked member of staff who'd been wiping down the countertops when I entered. "Now," I ground out when they remained frozen in place, staring at me.

"Ice. O-of course, Dr. Wilder."

"It's for a head injury. A small bump," I added, in case they decided I should follow first aid procedures. There was no way I could explain what had happened, and so the ice would do. It *was* only a small bump, but my sunshine boy was in pain, and I needed to fix it.

Returning to my office with a bottle of water and ice wrapped in a clean dishcloth, I found JJ slumped in my chair, his head in his hands.

My stomach hurt all over again. Making sure the door was locked properly this time, I made my way over to him. Yanking my desk drawer open once again, I grabbed a blister pack of paracetamol and placed it on the floor along with the bottle of water.

"Hey. Come here." Lowering myself to the floor, my back against the wall, I held out my hand. JJ looked up, biting down on his trembling lip. His eyes were wide, and his lashes were damp. "Baby. Come here. Let me make it better," I said softly. He slipped out of the chair, climbing into my lap, and although he wasn't that much shorter than me, somehow, we made it work, his body curling into mine as he hid his face in my neck. Holding the makeshift ice pack to his head, I stroked up and down his back.

"I-I'm sorry." He sniffed, his body shuddering against me.

"I told you, it's not your fault."

"B-but Gage. He saw. He doesn't know about us." His voice cracked. "What—what if I've messed everything up for your promotion? I'm so sorry."

Now he was crying, trying to stifle the noises, and it killed me. My sunshine boy wasn't even thinking about the pain he was in, he was so worried about me. Swallowing around the lump in my throat, I brushed the hair away from his face, pressing a soft kiss to the crown of his head. "Listen to me. It's going to be okay. I'll talk to Gage and set things straight. He...he knows I'm bisexual, and so does Stuart—

not that I think he'll even say anything to him—so that part won't be a surprise. Yes, it wasn't ideal that he walked in on us, and to be honest, he's probably wishing he had some brain bleach after seeing me in such a compromising position, but he would never use it against me." I gritted my teeth, thinking about the awkward conversation to come. "He'll probably give me a warning, which I suppose I deserve, but I promise you, you've done nothing wrong, okay? You haven't messed anything up. Now, tell me, how's your head? I got you some paracetamol."

With a sigh, he lifted his head, his eyes downcast. I made sure to hold the ice pack in place as I leaned forwards to place a kiss to his cheek.

"Are you sure I haven't messed things up?" he said in a small voice.

"I'm positive. I trust Gage." Wiping away the tracks of his tears with my thumb, I smiled at him. "Come on, drink your water and take these tablets. Is the ice helping?"

With shaking hands, he opened the water and popped two pills from the blister pack, swallowing them, and then he curled back into me again, winding his arm around my waist. "It's helping. Thank you. For looking after me."

"Always," I promised, and I meant it.

"This can't be comfortable for you, sitting on the floor like this."

"Don't worry about that. I want to make sure you're okay." I kissed him again, this time on the lips, and finally, his mouth curved upwards into a small smile.

"You have a great bedside manner, Dr. Wilder."

"Now I know you're feeling better if you're making

comments like that." I grinned at him, and his smile widened. "There's my sunshine," I murmured, relief coursing through me.

"Thank you." Kissing me again, he rubbed his thumb across my jaw. "You should probably speak to Gage sooner rather than later."

Glancing at my watch, I grimaced. "Yes, I should. I have a lecture in forty minutes, and so does he."

JJ tugged the ice pack from my grip and climbed off me, rising to his feet. "I have a seminar then, too. No dancing for this one, just sitting down in a classroom. Will you text me afterwards? Tell me what he said?"

Standing, I pulled him back into my arms. "Of course I will. Please don't worry. It'll be okay."

He nodded, accepting my words. "Okay."

"What the fuck were you thinking, Kill? He's a student! If anyone other than me had walked in on you—"

"I know." Slamming my hand down on Gage's desk, I spat the words out. "I made a mistake, okay? I know that."

"It was completely fucking irresponsible. This isn't like you at all. Seriously, what the fuck is going on with you? You've never acted this unprofessionally before. You do realise the shit you'd both be in if anyone found out? You can kiss your two-year plan goodbye, for a start."

"I *know*." My entire jaw ached from clenching my teeth so tightly. "You're not going to say anything, are you?"

Gage sighed heavily, leaning back in his chair. "No. You

know I wouldn't do that. Promise me you'll never do that again, though. At the very least, lock your fucking door."

"We thought it was locked." I shook my head. "I won't be making that mistake again, trust me."

"You do realise I can never unsee that? I'm going to send you my therapy bill."

My jaw unclenched, just enough for me to realise how much tension I'd been holding. "I suppose that's the least I deserve."

"How long has this thing been going on between the two of you, anyway? Is it serious? He's...how old is he, Kill? Nineteen? Twenty? And a *student*."

"Of course I know he's a student. He's twenty. And I don't fucking know what it is. He's...fuck." Groaning, I scrubbed my hand across my face. There was no possible way to explain the unexplainable.

"Oh, wow." Gage's voice dropped a few octaves. "The heartless Dr. Wilder caught feelings for someone. I never thought I'd see the day."

"Fuck off."

"I'm happy for you, mate. I really am. But you have to admit, you didn't choose the easy option. This is gonna cause all kinds of issues when it gets out."

"Which it isn't because you're not going to say anything."

"Be realistic, Kill. You can't hide it forever. That's not fair to either of you. You need to decide what's more important to you. Him or the career you've been working for all your adult life. Not to mention, you could be putting his future in jeopardy. Obviously, I don't know anything about him, but I doubt future employees would look kindly on him having an affair with a lecturer at his uni."

He wasn't saying anything I didn't already know, but hearing it from someone else solidified it.

There was no future for me and JJ, no matter how much I wanted there to be.

TWENTY-THREE

KILLIAN

Stuart tapped my computer screen. "It says right here. I'm paraphrasing, but the application wording basically says a relationship with a student will disqualify you from the promotion."

"Thank you. I can read." My jaw clenched as I stared out of my office window, unseeing.

Gage exhaled heavily. "Kill. Listen. It's just John being stuck in the old ways, adding all the extra shit he doesn't approve of so he can make sure whoever gets chosen shares his values. I looked it up, and there's nothing in the rules that says you can't have a relationship with a student. That line he's added doesn't even mean anything. It's discrimination to stop you getting a promotion for that reason."

Spinning around, I took in my two colleagues. Stuart was seated at my desk, frowning at my monitor, and Gage was leaning against the wall, his arms folded across his chest.

"Me? Why would it apply to me? Why does it even matter? It's an irrelevant point."

They exchanged glances, and I hissed out a breath between gritted teeth. "If you have something to say, say it to my face."

Stuart cleared his throat. "Kill. We've noticed JJ coming to your office. All the time. And you're hanging around the performing arts end of the campus—we've both seen. He was there that night at the bar, too, wasn't he? We're just... we're looking out for you."

I sighed, defeated. "Gage told you what happened, then."

He glanced over at Gage, one brow lifting. "No, he didn't say anything to me. We discussed this last week. Is there something else I need to be aware of?"

"Gage can tell you if he wants to." Slumping into the chair at the side of my desk, I pinched my brow, attempting to stave off the headache that was threatening to make an appearance.

"Okay, well, he can tell me later. For now, let's get back to this application."

I'd read every line of the official application form for the professorship slash head of the business school when it had landed in my inbox on Monday morning. It had been put together by the outgoing head, John Saunders, and the vice chancellor had signed off on it. There were certain expectations that I knew I could meet, but one of the stipulations in the "no conflict of interests" section mentioned that having a relationship with a student wouldn't be allowed. It didn't specify whether it mattered if the student was from outside the business school, and I had the feeling that it wouldn't matter. If I continued this "thing" with JJ, I could kiss any hope of my promotion goodbye, which I'd been working towards for my entire career. It was a double blow after everything that had happened with Gage, making an already hopeless situation completely fucking impossible.

Stuart continued talking. "It also mentions that you're expected to set an example for the more junior members of staff. Reading between the lines, it looks like they want you to be seen at social events. The faculty dinner is going to be a big one. You need to be there."

"We knew that was going to be a sticking point," Gage interjected, and I glared at them both.

"Get out of my office."

Gage opened his mouth.

"*Now*," I ground out.

When they'd gone, I dropped my head to my desk. Once upon a time, my life had been simple. I got up, I went to the gym, I went to work, went home, and slept. Rinse and repeat. Now, everything was falling apart.

My inbox gave a soft ping, and I raised my head with a groan. There was a new email from the vice chancellor.

FROM: thomasstjames@lsuniversity.ac.uk
    TO: LSU Business School Staff
    REPLY-TO: vc-secretary@lsuniversity.ac.uk
    SUBJECT: BS Spring Faculty Dinner Confirmed Date

Hi All

. . .

Please find attached the business school faculty dinner official invitation with final confirmed date, time and location. You may bring a plus-one—please indicate in your reply.

Reply to vc-secretary@lsuniversity.ac.uk by Friday 4 p.m.

Looking forward to seeing you all there.

Best,
    Thomas

Prof. Thomas St James | BSc (Hons), PhD, FREng
    Vice-Chancellor
    London Southwark University

Attached was an invitation with the date, time, and location of the spring faculty dinner.

Gritting my teeth, I quickly tapped out a reply in the affirmative, stating that I was attending and wouldn't be bringing a plus-one, and then closed down my computer. It was time for my next lecture, and I couldn't allow my worries to distract me while I was teaching.

Arriving in the lecture hall, I spotted Ander Loveridge

and Elliot Clarke in the front row. My brows rose—seeing either of them anywhere close to the front was unusual, particularly Loveridge, who went out of his way to sit as far away from me as possible. As I eyed them with suspicion, they were joined by Preston Montgomery III and Liam Holmes, another two of my students who had a preference for the rows towards the back of the lecture theatre. All I could do was hope they weren't planning on doing anything disruptive, because after the events of this morning, I held a tenuous grip on my temper.

I did my best to tune them out as I prepared my slides and began the lecture, but when it reached the point of the students splitting into small groups to discuss the material, Ander slid out of his seat and made his way over to me.

"Uh, Dr. Wilder."

"Yes?"

He stared down at his hands. "It...fuck. This is gonna sound really inappropriate, but I know about you and JJ. It was an accident that I found out," he rushed out, "but I'm worried about him. Did something happen between you? He seems a bit sad. It's not like him."

My anger at Loveridge's impertinence was immediately replaced with concern. "Sad? How?"

He shrugged. "Maybe sad isn't the right word. He's... listless. It's hard to describe. Maybe most people wouldn't notice, but living with him, it's kind of obvious. It's like he's lost some of his spark, I guess."

"Since when?"

"Uhhh..." Tapping his chin, he thought about it for a moment. "Four days, probably."

Four days. Ever since Gage had caught us in my office.

We hadn't seen each other in person, although I'd texted him to reassure him, and that was down to me. I hadn't wanted to see him, not when I was so twisted up by what my heart wanted and what my head told me was the right thing to do.

"Fuck," I muttered. "Okay." Forcing myself to meet Loveridge's gaze, I managed to add, "Thank you for telling me, Ander."

His eyes widened dramatically. *Ander*, he mouthed, and I almost smirked. Almost.

"Does this mean I can call you Killian?"

My eyes narrowed. "Don't push your luck. Go and sit back down. I'll talk to JJ."

"Yes, sir." Giving me his usual salute, this time accompanied by a relieved smile, he backed away from me and returned to his seat.

The last thing I wanted was to hurt JJ. It was time I paid him a visit so we could speak in person.

TWENTY-FOUR

JJ

"Good job!" I pulled Alyssa and Leo into a hug. "I can safely say we're ready for our performance ahead of the showcase."

Throwing myself into preparing for the dance showcase was exactly what I needed when I was so unsure about everything that was happening with Killian. And speaking of the showcase...

"Before I forget—did you see the email with the showcase date and time?"

Leo bit down on his lip, his cheeks flushing. "I saw it in my inbox, but I was too scared to read it. D-do we have to perform for an audience?"

I rubbed his back soothingly. "You can do this, babe. Me and Alyssa will be with you for the group performance, and when you do your solo, we'll be right there in the wings to support you. If you want, we could round up a few friends for a rehearsal. What do you think? If you've already performed for an audience once, it won't be so daunting when you do it again."

He nodded slowly. "Um…yes. Okay. Thank you. C-can we make it a small audience, though?"

"Leave it with me. When do you want to do it? Today? It might be better to get it out of the way."

His eyes widened, a panicked expression crossing his face, before he sighed. "Okay. Let's do it. If you think it'll help."

"Aly? Want to do it?"

She waved her phone at us. "Already on it. The performance studio's free at 6:oo p.m., so I'm booking it now. I'll text Erin and Amy, see if they can come and watch. They might need some bribery to come out, though."

"I'll invite Ander, see if he can round up some of the football team. That should give them enough incentive." Glancing at my phone, I thought for a minute. "Okay. We have three hours. Want to take a break, have a snack and a drink, and we can reconvene in half an hour?"

All in agreement, I headed over to my bag to get my own phone. Time to see who I could round up for our performance.

As soon as I unlocked my screen, I noticed the unread message from Killian, and my heart skipped a beat.

KILLIAN:

Are you available later? I have a number of things to finish up in my office, but I'll be free from 7

Yes. Yes, I wanted to see him. Badly. We hadn't seen each other since Gage had walked in on us, and I needed to see his face, to know everything was okay. Not just to hear it over a text, but to look into his eyes and know he was telling me the truth.

And I missed him.

ME:

OK. I'll be in the Shaw performance studio.
Meet outside at 7?

KILLIAN:

You're studying late?

ME:

Showcase rehearsal

KILLIAN:

I'll meet you there, unless I'm running late.
If so, I'll text you

ME:

Looking forward to seeing you

KILLIAN:

Me too

He was looking forward to seeing me. A smile tugged at my lips as I exited out of my texts and scrolled through my contacts to Ander's name. After a quick call, I had the assurance that he'd show up with Elliot and at least one of the football team members. My second and final task was to send a quick message to my group chat that included Niccolò, Dexter, and Shay to see if any of them were free. That done, I sat back against the mirrored studio wall with my legs outstretched, sipping from my water bottle while I crunched on an energy bar.

Leo wandered over and took a seat on the floor next to me, his arms encircling his knees. "I asked Connor and Niall if they could come. They're, um, my friends from computing. Connor's busy, but Niall said he'd come. I...it's going to be weird, doing this in front of him."

"Connor? He's the one with the YouTube channel, right?" Before Leo could reply, I shook my head. I was getting off track. That wasn't important right now. The most important thing was to reassure him. "Listen. If your friend's coming, then it's because he wants to support you." I gave him an encouraging smile. "We're all here to support you. You've got this. I know you do. You've got the talent, and you know the steps."

He sighed, burying his face in his arms. "I-I wish I wasn't like this."

"Don't wish you were different. You're great as you are, babe. And you're not going to let anything stop you from blowing the minds of our audience with your talent, okay?"

"Okay."

"Good." Squeezing his shoulder gently, I finished up my energy bar and then leaned my head back against the wall. With the silence that had fallen, I found my thoughts drifting towards Killian again.

He'd reassured me by text that Gage wouldn't say anything about what had happened, but I couldn't help feeling like there was something he wasn't telling me.

Tonight, we'd speak properly, and I'd find out if there was anything he was hiding.

Our agreed rundown for the rehearsal was our three solo dances—Leo going in between Alyssa and me so he didn't have to wait for too long—and we'd finish up with our group routine. Strutting onto the stage to introduce us, I glanced down at our audience.

Alyssa's dancer friends, Erin and Amy, were in the front row. Next to them, my housemates Ander, Elliot, Levi, and Charlie had all shown up, and they'd dragged my least favourite member of the football team with them, Finn. Niccolò was seated in the centre, and he waved madly when I caught his eye. I blew him a kiss, making him grin. The group was rounded off by Leo's friend Niall, which meant that Leo only had nine people to dance in front of, excluding Alyssa and me. Perfect.

After intros, I dimmed the lights as much as possible and turned the stage lights' brightness up, plunging the audience into shadow to help Leo feel more comfortable.

Then, we began.

Alyssa's dance went off without a hitch, and she was rewarded with enthusiastic applause and whistles from our audience. After taking a bow, she skipped over to the side of the stage, where Leo was waiting with me.

"You can do it." She squeezed his arm, smiling widely. "It's such a buzz, honestly."

He gave her a jerky nod, and then with a deep breath, he stepped onto the stage. From my vantage point, I could see his whole body shaking, and all I wanted was to comfort him, but he had to do this for himself.

The music started up, but instead of starting his routine, he remained frozen in place, his eyes wide and fearful.

Fuck.

"Do something!" Alyssa hissed in my ear. "Quick!"

Sweeping my gaze across the stage, I came to a decision. "I'm gonna turn the spotlight right down and put the sidelights on low. When I'm done, restart the music, okay?" Without waiting for a reply, I sprinted towards the lighting deck, turning the spotlight to low and adding a soft glow from the sidelights. Leo blinked, and suddenly, the fear in his eyes was replaced by determination. This time, when the music started, he moved.

Alyssa clung to my arm, both of us holding our breaths as Leo danced. But he did it. He made it through the entire routine with only a couple of minor errors that I doubted anyone else would have picked up on.

When he came offstage to the sound of applause, there were tears in his eyes, and his body shook. "I did it. I actually did it," he whispered, his voice cracking, and we pulled him into a group hug, the three of us basking in this moment.

Pulling back, I smiled. "We never doubted you."

He returned my smile with a tremulous one of his own. "Thanks. Your turn now."

Right. I'd forgotten I was up next in all the excitement.

"Please can one of you turn the spotlight back up? You know how much I love it." Shooting them a grin, I pulled my workout top off and strutted onto the stage in just my dance tights, dipping into a sweeping bow.

My theatrics were forgotten when the opening notes of my song began, and I was swept away by the music, moving through the steps seamlessly for the most part. When my routine finished, I straightened up, panting, before I took a final bow.

Wolf whistles and cheers rang out from our audience, and I blew kisses and took several more bows, playing to our minuscule crowd. The fun ended when Ander shouted at me to get off the stage, and with one final gesture—this time, my middle finger thrown up at my housemate—I left the stage.

After a quick water break, we performed our group dance, and Leo gave the best performance I'd seen from him despite his obvious nerves.

"You were amazing. Both of you." I grinned, pulling him and Alyssa into a group hug and kissing their cheeks. None of us could stop smiling, and I was so glad that we'd done this.

When the lights came back on, Leo disappeared with his friend Niall, eager to escape. Charlie, Finn, and Levi waved goodbye before heading outside, and lifting my hand in acknowledgement, I strode to the edge of the stage, lowering myself to sit on the edge with my legs dangling over the sides. Alyssa caught my eye, giving me a bright smile as she headed over to her friends. "Good job, JJ. See you next week."

"Celebrate tonight, babe. You earned it." I blew her a kiss, and she returned the gesture as her friends threw their arms around her, the three of them following the others through the exit.

Then it was just me, Ander, Elliot, and Niccolò remaining. Leaning back on my hands, I stretched out my legs. "Thanks for coming. I owe you. Drinks are on me next time we go out."

"You were amazing." Elliot smiled at me. "I mean, I knew you were already, but those two dances were just... you were great. Your friends were, too."

"They were, weren't they?" I returned his smile,

replaying Alyssa's and Leo's moves in my mind. They'd both surpassed themselves tonight.

"I guess I can concede that you're the better dancer out of you and me." Ander sighed heavily, and I could see him trying to fight a grin. "But I do have natural talent."

"You do, and you look good in my gold shorts." We smirked at each other while Elliot rolled his eyes at us both. The truth was, I knew Elliot very much appreciated seeing his boyfriend in my booty shorts. He practically drooled every time Ander helped himself to anything from my superior wardrobe.

"Oooh...JJ." I turned to see Niccolò shooting me a sly grin. "Your hot doctor's here."

"Don't you start calling him that, too. It's bad enough when G—" My words died in my throat, my mouth falling open as my brain caught up with what he'd just told me. "*What the fuck? Where?*"

He nodded towards the door, where an incredibly handsome man dressed all in black leaned against the wall, his hands shoved into his pockets. When he saw me notice him, his lips curved into a hint of a smile, those gorgeous ice-blue eyes fixed on mine, and a whole horde of butterflies took flight in my stomach.

"Oh," I whispered. But it was only 6:46 p.m., and I thought we'd agreed to meet outside. Why hadn't I thought any of this through?

"What the fuck? Ander! That's Dr. Wilder!" Elliot was elbowing Ander, and Ander was muttering something to him, but I paid them no attention, jumping off the stage and heading straight for Killian.

When I reached him, I suddenly remembered that I

was shirtless and sweaty from dancing, and I came to a halt, glancing down at myself. "Uh...sorry. I've been dancing, and I'm all sweaty—"

His hand came out, gripping my wrist, and he yanked me into him. "I don't fucking care," he growled, his lips coming down on mine in a hard, possessive kiss.

He was kissing me in front of his students.

Ripping my mouth away from his, I stared at him, wide-eyed and panting. "Kill. Your *students*."

"I know." Glancing over my shoulder, he smirked as he took in what I was sure was a range of shocked expressions. "Let's see...your friend Niccolò knows about us, thanks to your grandmother. Loveridge knows, and I assume Clarke does, too, since he's attached to Loveridge's hip."

I swallowed. "Can you please call them by their first names?"

His gaze flicked to mine, his mouth twisting into a grimace, but eventually, he nodded. "I suppose so. But just for you."

My entire body warmed. "Just for me?" Wrapping my arms around his shoulders, I placed a soft kiss to his jaw. "Sorry I'm not prepared. Are you okay waiting here while I have a quick shower?"

When he nodded, I stepped back from him. Spinning on my heel, I turned to face my three friends. Ander wore a look of resignation, Elliot seemed like he was still in shock, and Nic was grinning at me.

Arms wrapped around my waist from behind. "I'm rather enjoying the look on your friends' faces."

"You're sadistic," I muttered, leaning back into him.

"So they say. But not with you. Did I mention how delicious you look in these dance tights?"

"Don't you dare make me get an erection in front of my friends. You're lucky I'm wearing a dance belt under these tights." Pulling away from the ridiculously tempting man who was chuckling darkly behind me, I moved in the direction of my bag. What was up with Killian today? He seemed to be fine with physical affection in front of his students, which was *not* what I expected. At all.

Niccolò stopped me. "JJ! I just got a text from Dex to say they're doing two-for-one cocktails at Revolve tonight. Are you coming out with us?"

"You should go."

I stiffened at the low voice behind me. What the fuck? Killian had come here to see me—we'd even prearranged it —and now he wanted me to go?

"Really? I thought we were going to spend time together."

"We will. But I'm not going to take you away from your friends."

That niggling feeling that something was wrong was back, but I did my best to push it down. Instead, I shrugged. "Maybe. We can talk about it later. I'll be back as quickly as I can."

TWENTY-FIVE

KILLIAN

When JJ left the studio, a heavy silence fell. I wasn't sure who was the most uncomfortable. Me or my two students, who were no doubt seeing me in a whole new light after my little display with JJ. Loveridge's—no, *Ander's* words about JJ acting listless and unlike himself had stuck in my mind, though, and the second I'd seen him onstage, looking so beautiful, dancing with fluid, graceful movements alongside Alyssa and Leo, the only thought remaining was that I wanted to tell him that he had nothing to be worried about. Not only that...I wanted to show him he was mine. Even though it could only ever be temporary. And that was why we needed to talk. To lay our cards on the table.

"This is awkward!" Niccolò said brightly, giving me a wide smile. "So. Ander and Elliot are your students. And they live with your boyfriend. So awkward!" He collapsed into laughter, and after a minute, Ander joined him.

Folding my arms across my chest, I rolled my eyes at

them both. "He's not my boyfriend." No matter how much I wanted—no, it didn't matter what I wanted.

Niccolò's laughter instantly stopped. "Not your boyfriend? What are your intentions with my bestie, then? You'd better not hurt him." Stepping up to me, making himself as tall as possible—which was still significantly shorter than I was—he placed his hands on his hips, glaring daggers at me.

"That's between me and JJ." With a sigh, I continued. "But you have my word that I will never knowingly hurt him."

He nodded, holding out his hand. I raised a brow.

"We have to shake on it. You agree not to hurt him, we shake hands, and then it means you can't break the agreement."

Right. Unfolding my arms, I took his hand, shaking it firmly. For some reason, he held on much longer than was socially acceptable, pumping my arm up and down. When I was finally able to retrieve my hand, a smirking Ander took his place. Wonderful.

"You'd better shake on the agreement with me, too. JJ's not only my housemate, he's my co-parent. His well-being is very important to me, Killian."

I gritted my teeth at his use of my first name, and he grinned.

"Co-parent?" I ground out against my wishes, my curiosity getting the better of me.

"Yep. We share custody of a snail called Sid." Before I had a chance to reply, he whipped his phone out of his pocket, proceeding to scroll through several photos of what appeared to be a Giant African land snail. Somehow, this extremely bizarre moment lightened the atmosphere, and by the time he put his phone away, my jaw had unclenched, and my shoulders had lost tension I hadn't even realised I'd been holding. When he held out his hand, I took it without hesitation.

"You're a good friend to JJ, Ander."

His jaw dropped, but he recovered quickly. "Thanks. Fuck, this is gonna take a while to get used to."

"You're telling me," I muttered. My sunshine boy's face flashed in my mind. He was worth every single one of these awkward moments. "I suppose you can refer to me by my first name, if you must. *Outside* of lectures."

"I'll take it. Hey, did you hear that, E? We can call him Killian now."

Elliot's wide-eyed, slightly panicked gaze flew to mine. I couldn't help the smirk from tugging at my lips.

"I hope you're not terrorising my poor friends, Dr. Wilder."

I turned, a helpless smile spreading across my face as JJ came to stand at my side. His hair was still damp from the shower, and he smelled delicious.

"Me? Terrorising your friends? I think you have me confused with someone else."

He arched a brow at me. "Oh, really? There's another LSU lecturer with the same name and reputation as you, is there?"

"Joshua. Behave."

A slow, dirty grin curved over his lips. "Maybe I don't want to."

"Fuck me. I didn't get it, but I do now." Elliot's awed

voice sliced through the sexual tension swirling between us. Clearing my throat, I took a step back.

"Get what?" JJ stared at his housemate.

His cheeks flushed. "Um. The attraction. That was hot."

"Dr. Wilder? I guess if you ignore his personality, he *is* hot," Ander mused.

"Thank you for that wonderful compliment, Mr. Loveridge. Who knew you were such a charming young man?"

"You would if you dropped the Mr. Asshole act," he shot back, and surprise of all surprises, I found myself grinning at him. He returned my grin with enthusiasm. "See! I knew you couldn't resist my charms forever. Soon you'll be begging me to call you Kill or—oh! Maybe we'll give each other nicknames."

"Don't push your luck," I growled, although there was no malice in my tone.

"This is so weird," Elliot mumbled, and I wholeheartedly agreed with the sentiment.

Niccolò suddenly gasped, drawing everyone's attention. "JJ! Now Killian has our approval and G loves him, can I call him Daddy?"

"You absolutely fucking can't," I said.

"Daddy? Why? And no!" JJ's emphatic disapproval had me smiling until he added, "Not in front of him, anyway."

"But he's like a daddy. The sexy kind, not the other kind."

Pinching my brow, I prayed for this nightmare to be over.

"Nic, don't tease him." The humour had disappeared

from JJ's voice, and Niccolò must have realised he'd taken things too far. The next thing I knew, he was throwing his arms around my waist and pouting up at me, all huge eyes and fluttering lashes.

"I'm sorry. Please don't be offended. It's just your dominating presence. You're so big and strong, and you're giving off all these protective vibes. It's sexy."

I had no idea how the fuck I was supposed to respond. Was he expecting me to hug him back? What could I even say in reply other than "what the fuck"?

A warm palm stroked down my bicep, and JJ pressed a soft kiss to my shoulder before gently disentangling Niccolò from me. He wrapped an arm around his friend, giving him a reassuring smile. "It's okay, babe. We know you meant it as a compliment."

We. I liked the sound of that far more than I should.

And I couldn't help admiring how JJ had instantly known what to do. This man was so fucking special. One in a million.

"You really like him, don't you? The way you look at him. That's the way I look at Elliot."

It was difficult to tear my gaze away from JJ, who was speaking quietly to Niccolò while stroking his fingers through his hair, but when I did, I found both Ander and Elliot staring at me in what appeared to be wonder.

"Yes, I do. Very much."

"Wow," Elliot breathed.

Wow, indeed.

JJ curled up on the ancient leather sofa, making himself at home. We'd gone to a small out-of-the-way pub that wasn't too far from campus but was rarely frequented by students or staff due to the somewhat overpriced drinks. In our hidden corner, soft murmurs of conversation drifting around us, we were in our own small bubble, just the two of us. As he delicately sipped from his wine glass, I found my hand sliding onto his leg. I just wanted to touch him.

He smiled when I gently squeezed his thigh, but his smile soon dropped. Placing his glass down on the pitted wooden table, he turned to me. "So. We need to have a conversation."

"Yes. We do." A ball of dread sat heavy in my stomach. There was a chance—a big one—that when JJ heard what I had to say, it would mean the end of us. In the studio earlier, I'd almost felt hopeful, getting the grudging approval of his friends and being openly affectionate in front of them. But the truth was, nothing was ever going to be that simple for us. Not after what I was about to tell him. Not when he was a student and I was a teacher. Not when he was so young and free and happy and I was older and jaded. Maybe I'd always been that way. Jaded. But JJ had brought light into my life and shown me a different path. I'd be forever grateful to him for that.

Fuck, I didn't want to do this. Every part of me rebelled against it, in fact. But I had to. I owed it to him to be completely upfront and honest. It was a risk I needed to take, for both our sakes.

Steeling myself, I began. "I spoke to Gage. Then I had an email..."

I laid it all out as clearly as possible, sticking to the facts.

When I'd finished, he remained quiet, contemplating my words.

Eventually, he spoke. "Okay. Here's how I see it. This is your career. It's important to you, and I'd never stand in your way. I appreciate your concerns for me and my future career, but honestly, I don't think that's an issue." He swallowed hard, clenching and unclenching his fists, and it was so fucking painful to see him distressed because of me. "What *is* an issue is your promotion. We can't do anything to jeopardise that. I'd never forgive myself, and we'd end up resenting each other. So I think...I think it's best if—if we end things between us."

Fuck. Even though, deep down, I'd known this was inevitable, the pain was almost unbearable. My throat became clogged, and I struggled to speak, emotion bleeding through my voice even though I did everything I could to push it down.

"I shouldn't want you, but I do. You're an amazing man, Joshua, and I don't want this to end. But I suppose...I always knew this had an expiry date. I knew I was never going to be able to keep you."

He gave me a sad attempt at a smile, his eyes brimming with unshed tears. One spilled over his lashes, and I fucking hated myself for making my sunshine cry. "I-I never thought it would last, either. I never thought there would be a future between us. I hadn't ever planned on a relationship, or even a situationship, or whatever you want to call this thing." Another tear ran down his cheek, and his bottom lip wobbled. "I just—I just never realised that ending it would hurt so fucking much."

"*Joshua.*" I couldn't bear his pain. Pulling him into my

arms, I held him tightly, doing everything I could to push down the tidal wave of my own emotions that was threatening to drown me. Only by knowing that I needed to stay strong for him did I manage. I could fall apart later when I was alone. JJ needed me now.

His tears soaked my shirt as I blinked away the wetness from my own eyes.

The very same day I'd made my promise to his friends, I'd broken it.

TWENTY-SIX

KILLIAN

The weather matched my mood. Unseasonably cold, grey, and drizzling. My mood soured even further when I reached the front of the queue in the coffee shop, and the barista recognised me, greeting me with a bright smile. "Morning! Your usual? An Americano and a caramel Frappuccino with whipped cream?"

Completely unprepared for the stabbing pain that resulted from her words, I gaped at her for a moment, before my mouth snapped shut, my jaw clenching. "No. Just the Americano," I ground out, hitting my debit card against the reader with far too much force.

There were no more of those ridiculously sweet, ridiculously overpriced drinks in my future. And no more ridiculously beautiful sunshine boys, with the power to warm even my ice-cold heart.

Fuck. It hurt. It had only been two days, and I missed JJ so much. We'd texted each other, keeping our messages short and simple, because neither of us could bear to completely close the lines of communication between us, but we'd agreed that it was best not to see each other face-to-face for a little while.

I hated being apart from him, to know he was no longer mine, but as I'd told him, I'd always known I'd never be able to keep him. I could only hope that one day the pain would fade, that I'd stop feeling as though a part of me was missing. And even more than that, I wanted him to stop hurting. I *hated* that he was hurting, and that I'd been the one to cause him pain.

By the time I entered the lecture hall, my mood had darkened even further, and my students bore the brunt of it. I retreated into myself, reverting to my cold, hard persona, where nothing and no one had the power to hurt me.

When the torturous lecture was over, and the students fled the room, I heard the mutters from the corridor.

"Fucking hell, that was brutal."

"What was up with him today? He was worse than he's ever been before!"

"I need alcohol after that, and it's not even midday."

"What an asshole."

Someone cleared their throat close to me, and I gritted my teeth, lifting my head. Ander was there, a smirk on his face. "Bad day, huh? Maybe you need some alone time with JJ to improve your mood."

"Get. Out."

His smirk disappeared instantly, his eyes widening.

"Get the fuck out. *Now*." I slammed my fist down onto the table, making my laptop rattle, and with a mumbled "Sorry" and another shocked glance, he left me alone.

When he was gone, I buried my head in my hands. Guilt, remorse—because my students really didn't deserve my wrath when they'd done nothing wrong—and despair swirled through my stomach, making me nauseous.

I guessed JJ hadn't told his friends that we'd ended things between us. Ander Loveridge was many things, but he wasn't heartless. We'd almost been getting on, the last time I'd seen him, in fact.

Fuck.

Opening up my email client, I scrolled through the list of my students' email addresses until I found his, and stabbed out a brief message of apology. Slamming my laptop shut, I lowered my head to the desk, closing my eyes.

I just had to concentrate on getting through today. Then sleep would come, and my real-life nightmare would be over for a little while.

Walking out of the campus library after returning some research journals I'd borrowed, I stopped dead.

Across the square, coming out of the student union, was JJ. His head was bowed, and he was wearing a charcoal-grey hoodie with the hood pulled up. *Grey*. I'd never once seen him in grey. I hadn't even known he owned any clothing in that colour. Even at a distance, I could see the downturned slant of his mouth and his defeated posture.

It *killed* me.

Someone knocked into my arm, and I blinked, stepping away from the library doors, my gaze never leaving JJ. It took me a minute to notice Alyssa was with him, holding an umbrella in one hand, the other pointing in the direction of the library.

Where I was standing.

As he lifted his head, our eyes met across the crowded square. Time seemed to stand still as we stared at one another, and anguish tore through me at the look of devastation on his face. It took everything in me not to go to him, to comfort him, to tell him he was fucking mine, and I'd do anything to put the smile back on his face.

His bottom lip trembled, and he spun away from me, normally so light-footed, but he stumbled in his haste. Alyssa went with him, her face filled with concern as she said something to him, slipping her arm around his waist. He shook his head in response, and her shoulders slumped, but she carefully angled her umbrella over them both and hugged him into her, resting her head on his shoulder.

Through the haze of pain that still held me in a chokehold, I found myself grateful that he had someone looking out for him. Someone to care.

JJ was loved by so many people. My sunshine would be okay. The smile would be back on his face before long, and then maybe it wouldn't hurt so much. As long as he was happy, everything would be okay.

I kept reminding myself of that fact as I walked alone through the cold, rainy streets of London, to my flat that wasn't a home.

TWENTY-SEVEN

JJ

utting on a brave face. That statement had never been truer. I went through the motions, talking and laughing and teasing, but inside, I'd shut down. My friends were usually perceptive, and the only reason I managed to get away with it was because by the time I arrived at Revolve, they were all well on their way to being tipsy, if not drunk.

The only reason I'd agreed to come was because we were meant to be celebrating Shay's upcoming overseas trip. He was going to be paid insane amounts of money to strut down catwalks and pose for photos in exotic locations. Tonight was his send-off, and everyone was in the mood to celebrate. Everyone except me.

Not that anyone knew. I hadn't told anyone that Killian and I had decided to end things because I hadn't even come to terms with it myself, and if I stayed in denial, I could almost pretend I hadn't had my heart shattered. Almost.

I downed my fourth shot of the evening, slinging my

arm around Niccolò's waist as he bounced on his toes next to me. "Cheers to Shay, living his best life!"

My friends all raised their glasses. The lights swept over us, the music pounding through my bloodstream, but I felt nothing.

I was completely numb.

"Going to the bar!" I shouted at my dancing friends, and without giving them a chance to reply, I turned away, letting the pasted-on smile slip from my face.

When I reached the bar, Tom, one of the bartenders, took one look at me and immediately motioned for Cole to come over and serve me.

He studied me, his brows pulled together. "You look like you need a drink."

"Yeah. I do. Whatever. Something alcoholic."

His brows flew up. "What happened to flirty JJ? And the JJ who has very particular tastes when it comes to drinks?"

"He's on hiatus." Slumping against the bar, I sighed. "Just bring me something strong. Please."

"Make him a Huxley." Cole's boyfriend appeared at my elbow. "And one for me, too."

"You named a cocktail after him?" I stared at Cole, and he shrugged.

"Yeah. Why, you want me to name one after you?"

"That's not happening," Huxley warned us both, and Cole smirked at his boyfriend before turning serious again.

"I'll make you both one. Extra vodka in yours, JJ."

When Cole leaned over the bar to kiss Huxley after sliding our cocktails over, I turned on my heel and left. I didn't care if I came across as rude; I couldn't be around people in love.

Not tonight. It hurt too much.

The cocktail was delicious, but it did nothing to help. Giving up on using alcohol as a crutch, I downed a pint of water and then threw myself into dancing with my friends, radiating hostility towards any man who dared to enter my vicinity.

Eventually, I couldn't take it any longer. Leaning over to Niccolò, I spoke in his ear. "Babe, I think I'm gonna leave now."

"Going to get pounded into the mattress by your hot doctor?" He made a gesture that was far too lewd for someone as sweet-looking as him.

No, far from it. But—no. Fuck it.

"Something like that, yeah."

Pulling out my phone, I booked an Uber.

Two o'clock in the morning wasn't the ideal time to be pressing the buzzer for Killian's flat, but I didn't care. I held my finger down until his angry growl sounded through the speaker, and it was the sweetest sound in the world.

"If you don't fucking stop that right this second, I'm calling the police."

"Kill. It's me."

The door to the building clicked, and I pushed it open.

When I reached his flat and saw him standing in the doorway, my numbness instantly melted away, all the pain

I'd been keeping locked inside me crashing over me all at once. I couldn't breathe.

My eyes filled with hot tears, and I ran to him, wrapping my arms around him tightly and burying my head in his shoulder.

"Baby," he whispered brokenly, shuffling backwards to bring me inside. The door closed behind us, and he tugged me over to the sofa, collapsing down onto it. I curled into him, breathing him in, feeling his heart beating beneath mine, his body reassuringly warm and solid where we were pressed together.

Lifting my head, I met his gaze, and the usual icy blue was replaced with the stormy depths of an ocean of feelings I could drown in. His eyes were rimmed in red, and I wondered if he'd had just as much of a horrible time over the last few days as I had.

"I'm sorry. I know I shouldn't have come. I just...I just wanted to see you. I miss you so much, Kill."

"I'm so glad you came." He took a deep, shuddering breath. Bringing his hand up to cup my jaw, he tenderly stroked his thumb over my skin. "This is so fucking hard. I know we agreed it was the right thing to do, but to tell you the truth, I didn't want this to end. Not yet. I *don't* want this to end yet."

Was he saying what I thought he was saying? "I don't want this to end yet, either." My gaze searching his, I whispered, "S-so can we keep going? Just a little bit longer?"

His eyes closed, and he nodded once. This time, my tears were tears of relief, of love, as the man I'd fallen for held me like I was something precious. Like I was his and he was mine.

I knew it would mean even worse heartbreak when we came to our inevitable end, but for now, I'd do my best to live in the moment and enjoy the time we had left together.

"My sunshine," he murmured, kissing my head. "I'm so sorry I hurt you."

I pressed my face into the crook of his neck. "We're both in this together, Killian. We always knew this was temporary."

His arms tightened around me. "I know. But I'm so sorry, baby. It kills me to see you hurting and to know you're going to be hurt all over again when this ends."

"It kills me to see you hurting, too." I pressed a kiss to his stubbled jaw, tasting my own tears. Or were they his? "I hate it. You deserve so much, Kill. You deserve to be so, so happy. I want you to be happy."

"Joshua." His voice cracked, and all we could do was hold on to each other. It was hopeless, and we were doomed, but we were in this together.

"Come on. Let's go to bed," he murmured after a long while, when my tears had dried and I was drifting, my eyes closed as I lay against his chest, caught up in the quiet intimacy between us. "I want to hold you all night."

"Okay."

He did as he'd promised. He held me all night.

And when the morning came, he was still holding me.

TWENTY-EIGHT

JJ

The sun was shining brightly, and the air was fresh and crisp in the way that only a spring morning can be. Sipping my caramel Frappuccino, I glanced over at Killian as we exited King's Cross station.

Butterflies took flight in my stomach as his lips kicked up at the corners, his hand reaching out so his fingers could slide between mine. He looked so gorgeous, so relaxed today in faded jeans, a fine-knit jumper in a soft, dark grey, and a pair of Nikes. There were tiny gold highlights glinting in his dark hair and stubble, catching the sun's rays.

So fucking handsome.

I returned his smile, and he brushed his thumb across the back of my knuckles. "Is this okay?"

"Holding hands? Very okay. More than okay. Perfect." I felt as if I was babbling, flustered by the effect this man had on me. I was feeling things that I'd never felt for another human before. Deep things.

Lifting my hand, he placed a kiss to the back of it before he released me with a sigh. "We probably shouldn't hold hands in public. The likelihood of anyone from campus seeing us is minimal, but it's still a risk." He was right, and that was why I didn't protest. We were doing our best to be careful in the time we had left together. We'd agreed that we couldn't risk anything else happening on campus, so I'd stopped visiting him in his office, and he'd stopped bringing me coffee—making up for it every time we met up away from LSU, hence the drink I currently clutched in my hand.

Steering us to the left, he lifted his takeaway coffee cup as if he could read my mind. "How's your dessert in a cup?"

"Delicious. How's your tedium in a cup?"

"Energising."

"Oh, really?" Making my way over to the side of the pavement, with Killian right behind me, I came to a stop in the shadow of a tall building. Glancing around us to make sure we were alone, I said, "I think I need some energy."

His brows rose, amusement in his gaze. "Is that so? In that case, I think I need some sweetness."

We were both on the same page. When he angled his head, his lips brushing over mine, I sighed. Nothing could be better than this. This man, a sunny day, delicious coffee, and kisses that made my knees weak.

After the emotional roller coaster we'd been on, we both needed this.

"Hmm. Maybe you do have a point about the sweetness." He licked across my bottom lip. "So good." My lips parted, and his tongue slid against mine, our mouths moving together, slowly and deeply. I lost myself in the taste of him, the feel of his body against mine, the warmth of his palm in my hand.

"I could kiss you all day," I murmured when he pulled

back. With a smile, he placed a final kiss to the tip of my nose.

"That sounds like something we should definitely do."

"Definitely." We began walking again, crossing a bridge over Regent's Canal and then down the steps to the canal towpath. Taking sips from my icy coffee, I took in the sights around us. Barges and small boats gently bobbed in the water, sending tiny ripples across the surface. The occasional cyclist passed us at a leisurely pace, and couples and small groups meandered along the path, some with dogs pulling at leashes, excited to explore. "This is so nice. Quiet. Relaxed. Away from the uni. I really like this, Kill."

"Yeah? This isn't too quiet for you?" Before I could reply, he shook his head. "I know. When I was first getting to know you, I thought...well, you have so many friends. You thrive in company, in social situations. But now I know you, and I know you need your downtime as well. It balances you."

I stared at him in shock. "Yeah, it does. I hadn't even realised that about myself. You...you know me so well."

We stopped next to a barge that doubled as a small floating bookshop. His lashes swept down, hiding his expression as he turned his head, fixing his gaze on the water. "You know me, too, Joshua. You know things about me that I've never shared with anyone."

My heart swelled. After another quick glance around to make sure no one was paying us any attention, I wrapped my arm around the back of his neck, pulling him close. I placed my mouth to his ear, pressing a soft kiss to his lobe. "Thank you for trusting me with your secrets."

He didn't reply, but he turned his head, kissing my cheek softly.

Since we were next to the floating bookshop, we decided to check it out, stooping to enter. Inside, it was warm and cosy, with dark wood and cushioned seating areas upholstered in faded fabric. Bookshelves lined the interior walls of the barge, and we spent a while browsing through the various books on offer.

Holding a hardcover clothbound copy of *Lady Chatterley's Lover*, I wandered over to Killian. He was flipping through a book, but when I reached him, he sighed, placing it back on the shelf.

"Decided you didn't want it?"

Glancing at the book in my hands, he cocked his head, and I answered his unspoken question.

"This is for G. It's her favourite book. She likes to collect different editions, and I know she doesn't have this one yet. So, what about the book you were just looking through?"

He shook his head. "I don't..." Trailing off, he scrubbed his hand across his face, his expression pained.

Balancing my coffee cup on the book and praying I wouldn't spill it, I placed my hand on his arm. "Kill. Tell me."

"I never...I had few possessions growing up and never any money to spare for, you know, frivolities. I suppose I'm not really used to buying things for myself. Things I don't need, at least."

Oh, fuck. It took me a minute to gather my composure, and then, straightening my shoulders, I cleared my throat. Thankfully, my voice came out steady, giving no clue to the way he'd shattered my heart with his words. This man deserved the entire world, to not feel guilty about spending less than a tenner on a fucking book. "Give me the book."

His gaze flew to mine, and I hardened my expression, letting him know I was serious. Eventually, he sighed, pulling the book from the shelf. He took my coffee and replaced it with his chosen book, *One Hundred Years of Solitude* by Gabriel Garcia Marquez.

"Good. Okay. Now we're going to go and pay for these. Or, more accurately, you're going to pay for your own book, and I'll pay for mine. You work hard for your money, Kill. You deserve to treat yourself."

"I'm buying the book for G," he said instantly, and the fact that he had no issue with buying things for someone else but he couldn't do the same for himself made me feel really fucking sad.

I let him pay, though, and when we were back outside in the sunshine, he seemed brighter, giving me a warm smile as he dropped his empty coffee cup into the designated bin. Drawing me closer, he placed a quick kiss to the side of my head, his smile widening as I turned to meet his gaze.

"Come on. Let's walk along the canal to Camden Market and get some lunch from the food stalls. What do you say?"

My smile matched his. "I say yes. But first, let's take a selfie. I want to remember this moment." When I'd snapped the photo of us, the canal in the background, we both studied the picture. "We look so good together, don't we?"

"We do," he agreed softly. "Can you send the photo to me so I have a copy?"

"Of course."

"I told you to slice the potatoes, Joshua. Do I need to do it myself?"

"Mmm, bossy Dr. Wilder makes a return. Please, sir, I don't know how to cut potatoes. Can you wrap your sexy arms around me and help me chop?"

"I'd spank you for that comment if you weren't holding a sharp knife," Killian growled in my ear, pressing up against my back. His big erection was a hard line against my ass, and I rolled my hips, just a little, teasing him.

He wrapped his hand around my hip, stopping my movements. "Behave. When this dish goes in the oven, we'll have thirty-five minutes to do whatever you want. Until then, behave yourself. It's difficult enough as it is for me to hold on to my control around you."

I pouted, just for effect, and he responded by chuckling and then kissing the side of my neck, making me shiver. Angling my head to the side so he could trail his nose up my throat, I reached my hand behind me, pulling him closer. "Can you show me how to slice the potatoes, please?"

We both knew that I was competent in the kitchen, but he went along with my little game anyway, wrapping one arm around me and sliding his other onto the countertop, his hand closing over mine around the knife handle. Together, we finished slicing and layering the potato with garlic-infused cream in the ceramic dish, and then Killian grated cheese on the top while I basted the chicken that was already roasting in the oven. The whole thing was an exercise in restraint, with my erection throbbing in my jeans and Killian shooting me heated looks from across the kitchen island, a dark promise in his gaze.

Finally, everything was in the oven, and we made the most of our thirty-five minutes, with Killian prepping me until I was begging for his big cock, then bending me over and fucking me hard and fast, working my cock at the same time, until I came all over his hand and the back of the sofa. When he finished inside me, we collapsed together, sated and breathless.

"How does it get better with you every time?" I wondered aloud. "I can't get enough of you."

Smiling against my skin, he pressed a kiss to my nape. "You know it's the same for me." With a groan, he withdrew his softening cock from me and helped me to my feet. "As much as I fucking love the look of my cum dripping out of you, we have four minutes before the timer goes off. Come on, let's shower before the food's ready."

Showering with Killian Wilder was never going to take four minutes. Not when I had his gorgeous body right in front of me, rivulets of water running over his muscles, his dark hair plastered to his head, droplets streaking down his face. It would take someone with iron restraint to resist him like this, and I did not possess iron restraint when it came to this man.

The water had run cold, and the food was overcooked by the time we'd finally finished, but it was totally worth it.

After our meal, curled up on the sofa with Killian, I flipped between scrolling through my phone and reading the latest issue of *Dance Europe* magazine, my reading glasses perched on the end of my nose. The flat was quiet, other than the muted sounds from the street below us, interspersed with the whisper of turning pages, with Killian engrossed in his new book.

"I love seeing you here in my flat."

Glancing up, I found Killian watching me, his book open on his lap. His gaze was so soft.

"Me too. Love being here, I mean. With you."

I wished we could stay in this moment forever.

TWENTY-NINE

JJ

"**G**wants to know if you'll come with me to see her today." I rolled over, showing Killian my phone screen. He rubbed his eyes, blinking against the sudden brightness, still waking up. His dark hair was all dishevelled, and he looked so sleepy and gorgeous. I loved that I got to be the one to see him like this.

"Yeah, okay," he said, his voice raspy. "When?"

Glancing at the clock on my phone, I calculated how much time we'd need. "Three hours? Maybe four at the most?"

Stifling a yawn, he nodded. "Three hours gives us plenty of time. Tell her yes."

When I'd tapped out a reply, he took my phone from my hand, placing it on his bedside table. Then, he rolled on top of me, stretching his body out over mine. "Hi."

"Hi," I replied breathlessly.

"I fucking love waking up with you in my bed." Lowering his head, he placed a chain of kisses across my jaw.

This man.

"I love waking up with you," was all I managed to say before he captured my mouth, and I was lost in him again.

Everything was perfect until breakfast. As I was finishing up my omelette, my phone buzzed, and when I opened it, I saw an email from the head of my dance degree course. Opening it up, I saw that we'd been given a schedule of events for our dance showcase, with the times for each of our dances. There was also a ticket link we could share with any interested parties, as the showcase was open to a wider audience.

"Second-year dancers... That's not too bad. My group dance is forty minutes into it. Then my individual one's close to the end."

In the middle of lifting a piece of toast to his lips, Killian stared at me, confused.

I rushed to explain. "Sorry, the dance showcase. I just got an email with all the timings so I know when I'm onstage."

"What date is it?"

When I told him, his entire face fell, and he placed his head in his hands with a groan. "Of fucking course it would be."

"Killian?"

Raising his head, he met my gaze, a resigned expression on his face. "It's the same night as my faculty dinner."

"Oh, my. You are in a bit of a pickle."

That was an understatement.

Killian had been his usual charming self with G, presenting her with the book from our date. He'd wanted me to give it to her, but I'd insisted he did, and the smile followed by the profuse thanks she'd given him was worth everything. We'd all had tea and crumpets together, and then Killian had left us, excusing himself politely so I could spend time on my own with my grandma. I hadn't wanted him to leave, but he'd been insistent, and I knew what was on his mind.

The email.

Which brought me back to my current conversation with G.

"We agreed that there would be an expiry date. It could never work out between us, not in the long run. Not with all the obstacles in our way. I guess…now we know what the expiry date is."

G sat in her armchair for a moment, wringing her hands before she stood, slightly unsteady. When I went to stand, too, she waved me away, as I knew she would. Picking up her newspaper from the table, she made her way over to where I was seated on the other armchair in her room.

Rolling up the newspaper, she drew back her arm and slapped me on the bicep with it. Hard. Who knew an eighty-two-year-old woman had so much strength?

"Ow!" Rubbing my arm, I attempted to make sense of what had just happened. "What was that for?"

"That was for you acting like a fool." When I stood, unwilling to let her remain standing for too long, she lowered herself gracefully into my vacated chair, holding eye contact. "It's clear to me that you love each other, Josh."

"Love?" I whispered.

"Yes, *love*. He's your one great love, isn't he?"

Fuck. Licking my lips, I forced the words out. Words that I knew were true, no matter how much I'd tried to deny them to myself. "He might be."

"There's no might about it. The very first time you mentioned him to me, I knew he was going to be special to you. I know these things. I've always had a sixth sense for them. Then, when I met him for the first time, it was clear that you were infatuated with one another. And when he came here again, and you danced together...well. Niccolò and I both agreed that you were deeply in love."

Nic had spoken to G about this? Of course he had, the interfering little fucker.

"That may be so, but we have to think of his career, G. I won't do anything to jeopardise that. Never. No matter what."

"My sweet boy," she murmured, a gentle smile on her face. "Your grandad would be so proud of you. *I'm* so proud of you. You're a wonderful man, Josh. Caring, kind, intelligent, talented...everything I could have ever hoped you'd be. My only wish for you is for you to be happy. That's always been my wish for you. I know you can be happy without your doctor, but you're much happier with him, aren't you?"

Swallowing around the lump in my throat, I nodded. "I...I love him, G. And I don't know what to do."

"My darling." She held out her hands, beckoning me towards her. "It will all be well. I promise you."

I hugged her close. "We agreed we'd end things. We even tried to end things once. But I...I don't know how to let him go." Tears filled my eyes yet again, and I angrily blinked them away. "I know I have to let him go. We agreed, and it's going to happen. This faculty dinner is a big deal for him, and if anyone found out we'd been seeing each other…it would ruin everything for him. At least if we have a clean break before that, he won't have to lie to anyone. He can get his promotion with a clean conscience, completely on his own merits, when everyone realises just how fucking amazing he is."

"Language, Josh." She tutted under her breath, shaking her head. "Listen to me, and remember my age. I've experienced many things in my lifetime, and I have a number of years of wisdom. Promise me you'll wait until the dinner and the showcase have finished before you make any drastic decisions about your relationship."

I sighed. "It's not just up to me. Killian has a say, too."

"Convince him, then. I know how persuasive you can be. Promise me."

"I-I guess I can ask him to wait until they're over. But even if he agrees, it won't make a difference. We'll still have to end things when he gets the promotion."

She gave me a small, enigmatic smile. "Maybe, maybe not. There's no harm in waiting, though, is there? The last thing you need is to upset yourself before such a momentous occasion." Rubbing her hands together, she directed her gaze towards the table. "Now, shall we play a game of cards while I tell you what Barbara said to poor George?"

THIRTY

KILLIAN

Smoothing down the lapels of my midnight-blue suit, I eyed myself in the mirror with a grimace. My reflection grimaced back at me, and I forced myself to take a step back and let a neutral expression settle over my face.

Midnight-blue suit. Black shirt with the top button undone. Plain pewter cufflinks. Polished black loafers. Hair perfunctorily styled. A neatly trimmed beard—because my stubble had grown in the past week, and I hadn't had any incentive to cut it. It was short, but it was arguably more beard than stubble at this point.

I looked the part, I supposed, but I didn't feel the part.

I was hollow.

This was potentially the most important evening of my career, and yet I couldn't muster up any enthusiasm. My head and my heart were both far away, stolen by a beautiful dancer who'd become my entire world.

Spinning away from my reflection, I headed out of the door and into the Uber that would lead me to my fate.

"Killian Wilder," I told the person manning the entry to

the event. They scanned the iPad in their hand before nodding and directing me inside.

Before I could reach the bar for a much-needed drink, I was stopped by John's hand on my arm. "Ah, Killian! Just the man I was looking for. I can't say anything officially, of course, not yet, but I hear congratulations are in order." With a wink, he nudged my elbow. I forced a polite smile, but the feeling of *wrongness* inside me was increasing by the minute, and for a minute, I couldn't trust myself to speak. Thankfully, John didn't seem to notice anything amiss nor expect a reply, instead, glancing around us at the faculty members and their plus-ones milling around the function room as he continued. "I must say, I'll miss these events when I retire."

I finally found my voice. "Excuse me for a moment," I gritted out, escaping in the direction of the bar. My phone buzzed softly in my suit jacket pocket, and I pulled it out.

It was a message from JJ.

JJ:

Good luck tonight. I'm so proud of you.
You're making your dreams come true

Everything coalesced all at once, and when I say it hit me like a fucking lightning bolt to the chest, I wasn't exaggerating. I staggered backwards, clasping my phone to my chest.

This wasn't my dream. Not anymore.

I had a new dream now.

And it was about fucking time I made it come true.

Scanning the room, I found the person I was looking for and headed straight for him. My heart was pounding, but my hands were steady, and I knew with utter certainty that I was doing the right thing.

Nodding politely to the vice chancellor's wife, I cleared my throat and then turned to the vice chancellor himself. "Thomas, could I have a quick word? In private?"

Surprise entered his gaze, but he inclined his head, and we made our way to the side of the room where we could speak without being overheard.

It was time. "Thank you for the opportunity, but I wanted to let you know personally that I'm withdrawing my application for the head of the business school due to a conflict of interests."

His mouth thinned. "And the conflict of interests would be...?"

Holding his gaze, I dropped the bombshell that could spell the end of my career. "That would be the fact I'm deeply in love with a student. Not one of my students, but still a student of the university."

"Ah. I see."

"Yes. Which brings me to my next point. Tonight is an incredibly important night for him, and I—well, I want to be there to support him. I apologise for my unprofessional behaviour, and I realise what the consequences of our relationship could mean for my career, but...I have to leave. Now."

"Ah. I see," he said again, his brows drawing together. "See me in my office on Monday. My PA will set up an appointment."

His ominous words should have filled me with unease, but all I felt was relief. I could deal with the consequences of my actions, and most importantly, I no longer needed to prove anything to myself. With a nod, I excused myself, heading straight for the exterior door. As I pushed it open, I swerved to avoid Gage, who was entering at the same time I was exiting.

"Kill! Leaving already? That has to be a record, even for you."

"Yeah. It's JJ's dance showcase tonight. By the way, I withdrew my application for the head of our department."

His jaw dropped. "You *what*? This makes no sense! What the fuck happened to you, mate?"

I shrugged, a grin spreading across my face. "I fell in love. I hear it makes people do crazy things."

"Fucking hell," he muttered, rubbing his jaw. "In that case...good luck. Say hi to your man from me. Oh, and tell him no more office blowjobs. Or at least lock the fucking door."

With a salute, I jogged away, leaving him shaking his head with a slightly confused smile.

Hailing the first black cab that showed up, I slid inside.

The driver turned to greet me. "Alright? Where to, mate?"

"The LSU campus, please."

THIRTY-ONE

KILLIAN

Reaching the LSU theatre, I encountered my first problem. No ticket. I had to hope my staff ID would get me inside, otherwise I'd have to resort to slightly more illegal methods.

"There you are, Killian. I've been waiting for you."

"*Glynis?*"

She smiled at my surprise. "Hello, dear. My, don't you look handsome tonight? Are you ready to go inside? We have front-row seats. My eyesight isn't what it used to be, you know."

What was happening? How did she know I was going to be here when I hadn't even known myself?

"I have our tickets." The man holding her arm patted his pocket with his free hand, and I realised that he was wearing the staff uniform of the retirement complex carers. "We'd better get inside so Glynis has time to get comfortable."

"Hush now, Bryn. Don't fuss. I'm perfectly fine."

I suddenly realised I hadn't greeted her properly, and

that wouldn't do. "Glynis." I lifted her hand and placed a kiss to the back of it. "You look beautiful."

"You charmer. I wore this dress when I sang for the American president many years ago, you know. He was rather taken with me, by all accounts."

Bryn coughed to disguise a snort of amusement, and a smile spread across my face. I loved JJ, and I suddenly realised I loved this woman in front of me. She'd nurtured JJ, helped to shape him into the amazing man I knew, and she was such a joy to be around. I was privileged to have her in my life.

Pressing a kiss to her cheek, I murmured, "Allow me to escort you inside."

As her arm slipped through mine, she laughed lightly. "Escorted by two handsome men. If only Barbara could see me now. Bryn, make yourself useful and take one of those selfie pictures, please. Make sure you get us all in."

Smothering a smile, he rolled his eyes but took out his phone anyway and snapped a picture. "Done. You know, this isn't in my job description, G."

"Neither is escorting me to a dance showcase, yet here you are. Could you send the picture to Barbara? Thank you."

"Always taking liberties, G. The things I do for you, I swear. I should get a pay rise."

"Pfft. You get paid plenty. Don't forget the chocolates I save for you every week, too."

I laughed at their exchange, glad to see that she had people looking after her who got her, who were genuinely happy to be around her. And who wouldn't be?

She coughed dramatically. "Need I remind you that I'm

on my deathbed? Do you want me to turn into a corpse before we get in the door? Hurry up, please!"

"I wasn't the one wasting time with selfies," Bryn pointed out.

"You took them with your phone, dear."

"Pay rise. Definite pay rise," he said as we finally began to move towards the door.

"What was that? I can't hear you. There must be something wrong with my hearing aid."

We reached the box office counter without further incident, and Bryn presented three tickets to the student volunteer while G announced to everyone in earshot that her superstar grandson was performing tonight. She was so proud, so happy, and if I'd had any doubts about my actions earlier this evening—which I didn't—seeing her like this would have wiped them all away.

The LSU theatre itself had two levels of fixed seating wrapping around the back of the room and down each side and a ground-floor level of removable seating to allow for a variety of performances. As G had already told me, our seats were in the front row, closest to the stage. We made our way down the aisle to the front of the theatre, and as I drew closer, I noticed several of JJ's dance students seated a few rows behind us. A few of them gave me shy smiles and nods, obviously recognising me from the class I'd attended as a spectator, and I returned their greetings. As the theatre filled, more familiar faces joined us. Niccolò, Dexter, Ander, and Elliot slid into the row behind me, along with a few of their friends.

Ander leaned forwards to speak low in my ear. "JJ told

us you were going to be at an important work thing tonight. But me and Elliot both thought you'd come."

"Some things are more important than work," I murmured, and he gasped.

"Please, please say that again, and let me record the business school's principal lecturer saying there are more important things than work."

"No."

He huffed but was thankfully distracted by even more of my students joining him. I had no idea JJ knew so many people in the courses I taught. It would make next week's lectures interesting, that was for sure.

If I had lectures to teach next week. The vice chancellor wanted to meet with me on Monday, after all.

Whatever happened, it was worth it to be here tonight, supporting the man I loved doing something he'd worked so hard on.

The house lights dimmed. The curtains opened, revealing an empty stage lit by spotlights.

Then, the showcase began.

I'd seen JJ's group dance a couple of times already, but seeing the three of them up onstage, the atmosphere electric with a full theatre audience, accompanied by all the lights and professional sound system...it was breathtaking. They danced so fluidly, and although JJ had confided in me that he was worried about Leo's nerves, no one watching would ever be able to tell. The three of them were confident and graceful, perfectly in sync.

When they finished, there was thunderous applause, and as they took their bow, I rose to my feet, cheering and clapping until my hands ached.

The next set of dances flew by, Leo and Alyssa blowing me away with their solo performances, and then it was JJ's turn. I'd never seen him perform his solo dance all the way through before, only a couple of short sections he'd practised when I was with him, but I knew just how many hours he'd put into it. This was the culmination of months of dedicated effort, and I couldn't wait to see all his hard work come to fruition.

Everything went dark, and then a single spotlight lit up the centre of the stage, revealing JJ dressed simply in black dance tights, on his knees, with his head bowed. When the first notes of the song began, he moved.

Softer beams of golden light swept across the stage, caressing his beautiful body as he undulated through a series of graceful, sensual movements, extending the long lines of his legs in what looked like balletic movements to my untrained eye. His torso shimmered with a subtle gold sheen, a muted version of the way he looked at Sanctuary, giving him the otherworldly vibe that had captivated me the very first time I'd seen him.

Extending his body into an upright position, he danced across the stage, so fucking poetic and beautiful that I forgot to breathe, caught in the spell he was weaving with his movements. He used every inch of available space, leaping and dipping and spinning, then dropping back down to the floor. Another series of fluid movements across the stage floor, and then he rose again to finish the final steps of his dance.

As the last notes sounded, the spotlights winked out until only one remained. JJ stood still, stretching out his body, extending his arms towards the ceiling and closing his eyes as he raised his head to light up his face with the final spotlight. There was a stunned silence in the audience when the final note died away, but then the applause came, and it was *deafening*. Leaping to my feet, tears filling my eyes, I clapped and clapped and clapped, completely overwhelmed by JJ's pure fucking talent.

"Oh, Josh. He shines onstage, doesn't he? Like a bright star." Smiling, G dabbed at her eyes with a tissue Bryn had whipped out of a small bag I hadn't even noticed he'd been carrying.

"Like sunshine," I said softly, aching.

My sunshine.

THIRTY-TWO

JJ

I was too impatient to take the time to shower and change. I was buzzing, high on adrenaline, eager to see what G had made of my performances. Most of the other dancers were of the same mindset, wanting to see family and friends. Backstage, I pulled on a soft canary-yellow zip-up hoodie, leaving it undone, jammed my feet into comfortable padded sliders, and then made my way back into the theatre.

There was G, beaming at me, her hand outstretched. I headed straight for her, wrapping her up in a hug while she told me how amazing I was and how proud she was of me. When I released her, she gave me one of her enigmatic smiles.

"I mustn't monopolise all your time. Not when someone else came all this way to see you."

"My friends can wait. They know you're my number one, G."

She glanced over my shoulder. "Ah, but I'm not talking about your friends. I'm talking about a certain doctor of yours, who, I dare say, was very taken with your performance."

What?

I twisted around so quickly I almost gave myself whiplash. Standing at the end of the row, leaning against the wall and looking completely fucking divine in his suit, was Killian.

My feet moved before my brain could catch up. When I was standing in front of him, I licked my lips, feeling inexplicably nervous for some reason.

"W-what are you doing here? Did the dinner— Was everything okay with the dinner? Are you okay?"

His lips curved into the softest smile, directed at me. "I left the dinner about five minutes after I arrived."

"Why?" I whispered, staring into his beautiful eyes.

"Because I realised that the things I'd once placed so much value in were no longer of value to me. My priorities have changed. I spoke to the vice chancellor and officially retracted my application for the head of the business school."

"I-I don't understand."

Reaching up, he cupped my jaw, gently drawing me closer to him. "Do you really not understand? Don't you know how I feel about you?"

I could only stare at him, caught in his intense gaze.

"Joshua," he murmured. "I don't want to live in a world where I don't get to call you mine. Where I have to hide my love for you when you deserve to be loved freely and openly. I don't want to compromise. I want you. You and only you. I've fallen in love with you, and I'm choosing you." His words faltered. "I...I hope you'll consider choosing me, too."

My entire body was shaking. "Is—is this real? You really love me?"

Sliding his hand around the back of my neck, he rested his forehead against mine. We were breathing in each other's breaths, as close as it was possible for two people to get. "You're my sunshine. You light up my life in ways I could never have imagined. I love you with everything I have." Taking my hand, he moved back, just enough to create a space to slide it between our bodies. He gently placed it directly over his heart, his fingers covering mine. "I give you my heart. It belongs to you."

I was struggling to wrap my head around his beautiful words, and I knew it would take a while to sink in, but this brave, wonderful man who'd just poured his heart out to me was waiting for a reply, and I wouldn't keep him waiting any longer.

Swallowing hard around the lump in my throat, I pressed my palm against his chest, feeling the beat of his heart underneath my hand. Brushing my lips against his, I spoke. My words were simple compared to his, but I meant them with everything that was in me. "Killian Wilder. If you're all in, I'm all in. I love you so much, and I choose you. I'll always choose you."

He trembled against me, and I wrapped my arms around him. When he kissed me, so softly and sweetly, I melted against him, kissing him back with everything I had. This man was mine. Properly mine.

"Your one great love."

We drew apart at the sound of G's voice, Killian gently

wiping a tear from my lashes.

"You were right, G." I turned to face her, leaning back against Killian as he slid his arms around my waist.

"I always am, dear, as you well know. You found your one great love in each other, and you made an old woman very happy in the process."

"You won't be happy after you see this text from Barbara." Bryn rolled his eyes, brandishing his phone. "She's sent back a photo of her posing with the three gentlemen from the third floor."

"That hussy! Right, places, everyone! Ander! Niccolò! Come here and bring your friends. We're going to have a group photo, with me in the middle, of course. Would any of you handsome young men like to show off your muscles? Ander, I know you would. Come, show the others how it's done."

Killian chuckled in my ear. "This is what my life is going to be like now, isn't it?"

I smiled, covering his hands with mine and sliding my fingers between his. "Afraid so. You get me, you get everyone else. I guess I'm a package deal."

"Is that so?" He pressed a kiss to the side of my jaw, lightly scraping over my skin with just a hint of teeth, a prelude for things to come later. When we were alone, far away from well-meaning but incredibly nosy friends and family. "As long as you're the only one in my bed, I think I could get used to it."

Tilting my head so I could meet his eyes, I found him smiling at me, his gaze soft. I returned his smile, my heart so full of love for him. "Good, because now I have you, I'm never letting you go."

THIRTY-THREE

JJ

The man standing between my legs had a look of intense concentration on his face as he carefully wiped the cotton pad under my eyes, removing the glittery black eyeliner from my lids. He'd removed his suit jacket and rolled up the sleeves of his shirt, but other than that, he was fully dressed, which was something I'd be rectifying just as soon as he let me get my hands on him.

I still couldn't believe what had happened tonight. It felt like a dream—the best dream I'd ever had.

"Do you have any regrets about turning the promotion down?" I had to ask.

Killian shook his head as he straightened up, padding over to the sink to dip a washcloth in warm, soapy water. "No regrets. I realised that I don't want it. I don't enjoy the social aspect, I already struggle with my work-life balance, and the promotion would only mean more work. And I have nothing left to prove to myself." He gave me a smile that was almost shy. "I don't need the promotion to prove that I mean something because, thanks to you, I've realised that I do mean something."

"You mean something to so many people, Kill. And you mean everything to me." I tilted my head up for a kiss, and he obliged, his lips curving upwards against my mouth, both of us so fucking happy.

He lifted the washcloth to my forehead, then paused, glancing down between us. "How are your feet feeling after tonight?"

I rolled my left foot experimentally. "Okay. Good, actually. But I wouldn't turn down a foot massage later, if that's what you're hinting at."

"Oh, I plan to massage a lot more than your feet." When my breath hitched at the dark promise in his voice, he gave me one of his slow, dirty smiles. But then he was back to business, taking care of me, just because he wanted to. Killian had such a big heart, and I couldn't believe he was mine. "Eyes closed, Joshua."

My eyes slid shut, and he gently dragged the washcloth over my face, cleansing it of my stage makeup. When he was rinsing the cloth, I spoke again. "Your work-life balance. You do realise that as part of my boyfriend-slash-partner duties, I'll be helping with that?"

"Boyfriend slash partner. Which is it?"

"Do you have a preference?"

Returning with the cloth, he swept it over my face again. "I thought I'd have a preference, but the truth is, as long as I get to call you mine, I don't care what other labels we put on it."

This man. "I fucking love you, Dr. Wilder."

"I fucking love you, my sunshine." He patted my face

dry with a soft, fluffy towel. "All done. We'll need to get in the shower for the next part. It's going to take a while to remove all the shimmer from your body."

Climbing to my feet, I shrugged off my hoodie. "You'll need to be very thorough."

Running a finger down the centre of my chest, he stopped at the waistband of my dance tights. "Believe me, I will be. Very, very thorough."

"You're going to make me come before we even get to the sex." I shifted on the bed, my hard, aching cock dragging against the soft towel Killian had placed underneath me. Killian's hands rubbing massage oil all over my body, plus the knowledge that he was completely naked, equalled one very sexually frustrated JJ.

And now I was thinking about myself in the third person.

"I can't think properly around you."

He laughed, sliding his hands down my back to my ass. "Believe me, I know how you feel. Spread your legs, baby. Let me see that pretty hole."

With a shiver, I obediently spread my legs, and he moaned.

"Fuck, look at you. Do you have any idea what you do to me, Joshua? How fucking hard you make me?"

I thrust backwards into his hands, and he kneaded the globes of my ass, never touching me where I wanted to be touched. "Kill, please. I need you."

"Already begging? You're so impatient, aren't you?" A

finger lightly circled my hole, then slid lower, pressing against my perineum. *Fuck.* My cock throbbed and leaked, desperate for some relief.

"*Killian,*" I fucking whined, rutting against the bed.

A hard smack landed on my ass cheek, making me cry out in surprise, a delicious warmth blooming across my skin. "Behave. Stay still, and I'll give you your reward."

"Fuuuck. Is it your big cock?"

Killian placed kisses over the area he'd spanked, and then he nipped me lightly. "Can you stay still for me?"

I doubted I could, but I'd try if it meant me being wrecked by his big dick. "Y-yes. I'll try."

"Good boy," he murmured, kissing lower. Then, his tongue was at my hole, and I was shaking with the effort of holding myself still as he licked and sucked and drew his teeth across the most sensitive parts of my skin.

"Fuck, Kill. That feels so good."

He raised his head, and I whimpered, so empty, *wanting.*

"I need... I need..."

"I know, baby. I know. You're going to finger yourself open now, okay? I'll be back." His weight left the bed, and I blinked, turning my head to see him standing, staring down at me, his thick cock jutting out, making my mouth water.

"Let me taste you. *Please.*"

He swore under his breath. "The things you do to me." I watched the precum beading at the tip of his hard length, and I slid my tongue across my lips. With another muttered swear word, he stepped closer to me. "This wasn't part of my plan, but I can't resist you when you beg so fucking sweetly. Roll onto your back, head over the edge of the bed."

I was half out of my mind already, and it was a relief to not have to think, just to listen to his gorgeous, low voice and follow his instructions. When I was lying on my back, my erection leaking precum onto my belly, he gripped the base of his cock.

"So fucking sexy," he ground out, fisting his hard length. "Just a taste, otherwise I won't last long enough to get inside you. Open up. Tongue out."

He fed his cock into my mouth, and I licked and sucked the tip, tasting his arousal on my tongue. With a groan, he pulled back, breathing hard.

"Fuck. That's enough, Joshua. I'm too fucking worked up. Get yourself ready for me. I'll be back."

Licking my lips, chasing his taste, I shifted back into the centre of the bed. I shoved a pillow under my hips and reached for the lube. Drizzling a generous amount on my fingers, I began opening myself up. When Killian re-entered the room, something clasped in his hand, I was panting, three fingers buried inside myself, my cock jerking and leaking all over my skin.

His gaze swept over me, his pupils so blown that only a sliver of ice blue remained. "Look at you. The sexiest fucking sight I've ever seen in my life. And you're mine. All mine."

Withdrawing my fingers, I moaned, so ready for him. I needed him so badly. "Come here. Please."

Crawling over me, he leaned down, swiping his tongue across my lips, and a burst of cool mint tingled on my overheated skin. "Open up. Let me kiss you."

Our bodies pressed together, moving against one another, both of us lost in hot, deep kisses. My hands smoothed down Killian's strong back, feeling his muscles flexing beneath my palms. He kissed down my jaw, my throat, sucking and biting and licking. My mind registered a myriad of sensations—his heart pounding just as hard as mine, his precum smearing across my skin, the warm weight of his body, his mouth worshipping me.

Killian's hand slid down between us, and something cool and smooth wrapped around the base of my aching cock. I gasped at the sudden, new sensation.

"Adjustable cock ring," he murmured in response to my unvoiced question. Lifting himself up onto one elbow, he smoothed lube over his erection and then slid a matching ring down his length. "I want us to take our time when I get inside you. Tonight is special."

I'd never been more turned on in my life, but at his words, fresh emotions filled me. I loved this man so, so much.

"I love you. Show me how much you love me."

Somehow, I grew even harder as he worked his fingers in and out of me, teasing my prostate, until I was gasping and arching off the bed. Finally, he withdrew his fingers and eased his dick inside me, filling me so completely it brought tears to my eyes. Our kisses turned messy as we panted into each other's mouths, my hands moving down his back to grip his ass, our bodies growing hot and sweat-slicked.

We fucked for what felt like forever, until neither of us could take it any longer. Pulling out of me, Killian loosened his cock ring, removing it with a relieved groan, and then did the same to me.

"Oh, *fuck*," I gasped, staring down at my cock, soaked

with precum, oversensitive and hard as steel. I was going to come at the slightest touch.

He thrust back inside me, right against my prostate, and it only took seconds for me to explode, my cock jerking against him as my cum shot over both our torsos.

"Fuck, Joshua. *Fuck.*" His muscles tensed beneath my palms, and then he thrust again, groaning out my name, shuddering as he emptied himself inside me.

Completely exhausted, we lay there, struggling for breath, until eventually, he pulled out of me, rolling onto his back and tugging me into him. I placed my hand over his heart, stroking across his damp skin, and he pressed a breathless kiss to my hair.

Moving onto my side, I laid my head on his shoulder. "So. We've been officially together for less than a day, and you already got us matching rings."

He chuckled, running his hand down my arm. "Moving too fast for you?"

With a grin, I raised my head to meet his amused gaze. "There's no such thing as too fast. Not with you."

THIRTY-FOUR

KILLIAN

"Do you see my dilemma?" Thomas steepled his hands, eyeing me sternly from across his desk. "There's nothing in the rules that prohibits a relationship between a student and a member of staff, but there's no precedent here, and there will be those who have an issue with it. Particularly if you're the head of the business school. On the other hand, if I were to turn you down, it could be seen as discrimination."

Leaning back in my seat, I shook my head. "When I said I was withdrawing my application, I meant it. I no longer want the position." Clenching my fists, hidden from the vice chancellor's view, I inhaled and exhaled deeply, steeling myself to ask the only questions that really mattered. "Will my relationship affect my partner in a negative way if I continue to work here? Is it going to be a problem for my current position? Do I need to start looking for a position elsewhere?"

He sighed heavily. "Clearly, you underestimate your value to the business school. Your position is not in question. You will remain as principal lecturer, irrespective of your relationship status. With regards to your partner, in all likelihood, any negativity will be negligible. As I already mentioned, there will be those who see a relationship between a staff member and a student in a negative light, but as far as I'm concerned, you're both adults, and there's no conflict of interest. His chosen degree path has no crossover with the disciplines you teach." A smirk tugged at the corner of his lips. "As long as you're not going around flaunting yourselves on campus, I don't have a problem with your relationship."

Flaunting ourselves. "I can assure you, flaunting ourselves is the last thing we want to do." Hopefully, Gage would take our office blowjob secret to the grave.

"Good. We'll consider the matter settled." Glancing at his computer screen, he frowned. "While I've got you here... Since my preferred candidate has withdrawn his application, do you have any thoughts on a potential future head of the department?"

One name came to mind immediately, and I knew he'd be perfect for the role. "Stuart. He's reliable, he's a team player, and he thinks things through before he acts. Not only that but he's respected by everyone in the business school. He'd be a solid choice."

"Stuart, hmm?" A thoughtful expression crossed the vice chancellor's face. "Yes. Stuart. Right. You've given me a lot to think about. If you'll excuse me, I need to set up a meeting with John."

It was my cue to leave. Rising from my chair, I shook his hand, thanking him again. I'd been fully prepared to look for another job if he'd given me an ultimatum or disapproved of my relationship with JJ, but things had worked out even better than I could have hoped for.

Stepping into the sunshine, I headed for the performing arts block to give my boyfriend the good news.

Outside the building, I found two familiar figures in deep discussion. "A cupboard, JJ! What were you thinking?"

"I'm thinking you owe me some thanks. Bennett's really into you, from what Ander's been telling me." JJ grinned down at Niccolò, and my own smile spread across my face, happy because he was happy.

"Hmm. I suppose— Oh! Daddy K! Hi!" Niccolò caught sight of me, bounding over to me and giving me an exuberant hug.

Daddy K? I mouthed to JJ over the top of Niccolò's head, awkwardly patting his back, and JJ bit back a smirk, but then his expression turned serious.

How did it go? he mouthed back.

I grinned before glancing down at the person still wrapped around me.

"Niccolò. I told you not to call me Daddy."

He released me, pouting. "But—" He registered my stern expression and sighed loudly. "Fine. Anyway! I don't have time to argue about this. I have a date with my hot footballer. Have fun, lovebirds."

"What was all that about?" I asked as he strutted away after blowing us several kisses.

"Bennett. He's a guy on the football team Nic likes, so Ander and I gave them a little nudge. I think everyone deserves to be as happy as we do, don't you?" JJ gave me one of his sunshine smiles.

"Yep. Now, come here and kiss me, and then I'll tell you what the vice chancellor said."

"I assume from the look on your face that it's good news."

"Very." Sliding my arms around him, I pulled him into me. "I'll tell you all about it after you give me that promised kiss."

Gripping my shoulders, he angled his head forwards, our lips brushing in the lightest touch. "It's a deal, Dr. Wilder."

We kissed, bathed in sunlight, out in the open for anyone to see.

No more hiding. Now, everyone would know that Joshua James Everett was mine.

THIRTY-FIVE

JJ

"Ready?"

"Kill, I've been ready for three days now. Let me see."

Killian's warm breath skated across my ear. "I'm a bit concerned I've made too much of a big deal out of this. It's nothing much, honestly. It's just—"

Wrapping my fingers around his hands, I peeled them away from my eyes, blinking as I adjusted to the light.

Killian's once-sterile flat had become a home.

A collection of books in varying colours and sizes filled a shelf. A large potted plant stood tall next to the TV stand. The sofa had new cushions and a throw, and under the window...

"You like it?" Killian led me over to the gold brocade chaise longue, a creamy blanket shot through with threads of gold neatly folded at one end. It was the perfect height to recline on, looking out of the window at the streets below. "I asked G for advice, and she suggested one of these. I picked the colour because it reminded me of you. My sunshine. You can sit here and people-watch or whatever you want to do." He cleared his throat, shooting me a smirk. "Christen it, maybe."

"Christen it. Definitely christen it." Turning serious again, I took in the changes he'd made. The furniture he'd chosen with me in mind. "I can't believe you did all this. You made it into a proper home."

"No." He drew me into his arms, kissing me. "*You* made this place a home. From the very first time you were here, sitting right over there on my sofa in those ridiculous socks." Socks that I knew for a fact he loved to see me wearing. Leading me over to the shelves, he picked up a new framed picture, handing it to me. "Remember this?"

I smiled down at the photo that Bryn had taken of me, Killian, and G outside the theatre after my dance showcase. That day marked the beginning of our official relationship, and now I'd see this reminder every time I entered Killian's flat.

"I can't believe it's already been two months since then." Carefully placing the picture frame back on the shelf, I leaned into Killian's body. "And now I get to be on your shelf."

"That's not the only place." He led me into the bedroom, indicating towards his dresser. There was another framed picture here—the selfie I'd taken of us next to the canal.

"I love this picture. I love you."

Trailing his nose up the side of my throat, he placed a soft kiss just beneath my ear. "I love you, too. And just so you know, when the end of the semester comes up and you have to decide whether to renew your housing contract for another year, I'm going to ask you to move in with me. If you want to stay where you are for your final year, I'll be completely fine with that, but know this, Joshua. When you graduate, you will be moving in with me."

"Oh, will I?" I managed to rasp out, so fucking turned on by his decisive words and the way he was grinding his cock against me.

"Yes. You will."

Honestly? I couldn't think of anything better.

Pouncing on him, I pressed him up against the wall, taking his mouth in a hot, hungry kiss. He moaned, grasping my ass and slotting his leg between mine.

The buzzer sounded, and we flew apart, gasping.

"Fuck. I forgot. Fuck. You're far too tempting, JJ."

"Me? *You* are."

The buzzer sounded again, and Killian stalked over to the door, adjusting his prominent erection. When he reached it, he paused, turning back to me. "We're continuing this when everyone has gone. For now, make yourself presentable. Picture Gage catching us—his shocked face should do the trick."

"Everyone? Who's everyone? What's happening?"

I had my answers a few minutes later.

***

Looking around me as I stood at the kitchen island, prepping the ingredients for a communal brunch, I couldn't believe this was my life. Killian's flat was full to bursting. Gage, Stuart, Stuart's wife Rosa, Ander, Elliot, Alyssa,

Niccolò, and G were all here. Stuart had set up a card game, and he, Alyssa, Ander, and Elliot were currently engrossed, cards in hand. Rosa was flipping through Killian's new books, and Niccolò and Gage appeared to be bonding over talk of football, of all things.

Killian hit some buttons on his phone, and soft music began playing through the speakers.

He stepped up to G, holding out his hand. "May I have this dance?"

She smiled, tears of joy in her eyes as they waltzed slowly around the flat. I knew she was remembering, as I was, and I loved Killian even more for giving her this moment, a little reminder of the happy times in our past and, at the same time, creating a new memory with him in it.

They reached the island and came to a stop next to me.

"Josh. It's time you took your man for a spin." She kissed my cheek and then Killian's. "My two darling boys. I love you both so much."

Killian turned away, discreetly wiping his eyes, and I gave him his space, leading G over to the armchair and getting her settled in with a blanket tucked around her legs. One of the retirement complex staff would be back to pick her up in a few hours, but for now, we got to spend quality time all together.

When I returned to Killian, he was mostly composed, and I wrapped my arms around him, placing my mouth to his ear. "You're family, you know. Our family. *My* family."

"I've never had a family before," he whispered, burying his head in the crook of my neck.

I held on to him tightly, letting him know without words that he had a family now, and we'd never let him go.

A new song began to play, and he lifted his head to meet my eyes, his gaze so soft and full of love. My heart skipped a beat.

"Dance with me, my sunshine," he said.

KILLIAN

EPILOGUE

FIVE YEARS LATER

"I want you to have this." G pressed something cool and metallic into my palm, closing my fingers around it. When I opened my hand, I stared down at the tarnished gold band, my eyes widening.

"This wedding ring belonged to my husband. Now, I'm not one for sentimental value, nor do I expect either of you to use this in place of a wedding band of your choosing, but I'd like you to take it for Josh, for when you propose to him. Perhaps as a promise ring, or engagement ring, or whatever the fashion is these days."

My gaze flew to hers. "Propose?"

"I know it's been on your mind. JJ's too. He already introduces you as his husband to practically everyone you meet."

We both laughed. It was true. Every single time he mentioned it, a warm feeling of belonging spread through me. It was inevitable that it would happen. Marriage wasn't for everyone, but I knew how important it was to JJ, and it had become just as important to me, too. I wanted to be able to introduce him as my husband for real, to see him wearing my ring, to make vows of forever in front of our family and friends.

Even my business school colleagues called us husbands these days. Five years ago, when the departmental email had gone out, announcing Stuart's appointment as the next head of the business school, I'd braced myself for a barrage of questions regarding the withdrawal of my application. The vice chancellor had made it clear that I was to be treated exactly the same as any of my other colleagues in a relationship, and I'd been prepared to defend my love for JJ, but I'd expected there to be some issues. JJ was a student, after all, and we were both men.

Despite my concerns, there hadn't been any real need for defensiveness. JJ had quickly become popular among my peers. He could charm anyone with his sunshine smiles, and my colleagues had not only accepted our relationship, but I'd made real, significant friendships over the past five years. It helped that Stuart was running the business school, too. He understood when I needed time alone, and he never pressured me. Well...other than going behind my back and asking JJ to make sure I showed up at various social events.

I forgave him for his subterfuge, though. Those events were bearable when I had JJ by my side.

Coming back to the present, I swallowed hard, the significance of G's gesture hitting me. This ring had belonged to the man G always referred to as her one great love, and that meant it was one of her most treasured possessions. "Th-thank you, Glynis. It's...I don't know what to say. Thank you. I can't express just how grateful I am to you for everything."

"I should be the one thanking you, Killian. Having you as part of the family and knowing that Josh has someone so wonderful to share his life with delights me beyond words. Now, make sure you keep that ring somewhere safe. I want to hear all about the proposal when it's taken place. Did I ever tell you about the time a certain film star proposed to me at the BAFTAs? Love at first sight, it was. Of course, I turned him down." She paused, affecting a sad expression. "The poor man was devastated. I felt awful."

My phone buzzed, reminding me that I had somewhere I needed to be. I didn't want to leave G, but today was a huge day for JJ, and I needed to be there for him.

"My apologies, Glynis. I hate to cut this short, but I need to leave now if I'm going to be on time for JJ. I'll look forward to hearing the details of your mystery film star proposal next time."

"Of course, my dear. I look forward to hearing all about it. Tell him how proud I am of him, and I'll see you both tomorrow."

"I will." Climbing to my feet, I bent to kiss her cheek and, after a final goodbye, left the retirement complex, carefully pocketing the ring.

The first thing I saw when I entered JJ's dance studio was my future fiancé's sunshine smile, directed at me. Wrapping him in my arms, I pressed kisses all over his face, still just as obsessed with him as I had been when we'd first got together. He laughed, bringing his hands up to cup my cheeks so he could hold my head still and kiss me properly.

"Right on time. I can't believe they're going to be using my choreo in a West End show. The West End, Kill!"

"I never doubted it would happen." JJ was passionate, dedicated, and so talented. He'd thrown himself into his career, splitting his time between running his very own dance studio with the help of Alyssa and one of his former youth centre students and building a name for himself as a choreographer. Today was the opening night performance of a new West End show, and JJ had choreographed a group dance routine for a pivotal scene in the performance, as well as assisting with the choreography for several other routines. His name was listed in the show's programme, and I'd managed to get hold of an early copy, signed by the cast and crew, and had it framed for him. I couldn't wait for him to see it when we got home tonight.

But first, we had a show to attend.

"I know you never doubted. You've been my biggest support." JJ threaded his fingers through mine as we left the studio. "You kept me going, even when I doubted myself."

"And you kept me going. You still do. Remember how I was in the beginning? My whole life was work. I used to forget to eat."

"We work well together as a team, don't we?"

"We do." Tugging him to a stop at the side of the pavement, I kissed him again. "We balance each other."

"Perfectly." His tongue came out, sliding across his lower lip as he gave me a sultry look from beneath his lashes. "And let's not forget our sexual compatibility."

I leaned into him, speaking low in his ear. "If you

behave yourself, I might give you a reminder of our compatibility when we get home."

He shivered. "In that case, I'll be on my very best behaviour, Dr. Everett-Wilder."

A smile spread across my face. "Everett-Wilder? What about Wilder-Everett?"

With a shrug, he tightened his fingers in mine, resuming our walk. "I suppose we can discuss that when you propose to me. Maybe we'll toss a coin. Or have an edging contest."

"*Joshua.*"

"What?" Innocently batting his lashes at me, he bit back a grin. "It's a great idea."

"What am I going to do with you?" I muttered, and he gave up trying to hide his grin, his lips curving upwards until he was beaming at me, so bright and beautiful.

"What are you going to do with me? Let's make a list. First of all, you can strip me down and—"

"Joshua!" I clamped my hand over his mouth. "Remember we're in public."

Pulling my hand away from his face, he tugged me down the street, laughter in his voice. "I'd say sorry, but we both know it would be a lie."

My sunshine boy. I loved him so fucking much.

I pressed a kiss to his cheek. "You're lucky I love you."

His eyes met mine. "Yes, I am. And you're lucky I love you, too."

We crossed the road, our fingers entwined. He was right. I was lucky. What had begun as a one-night stand had completely changed my life in unimaginable ways. Everything was better now.

With him.

"There's the theatre." Stopping us in our tracks, I pointed down the busy street. From our vantage point, we could see the entirety of the front of the theatre. The show's title was emblazoned in sparkling golden lights over the entrance.

JJ stared at the building with huge, bright blue eyes, taking in the lights and the huge posters advertising the show he'd spent months choreographing. "I can't believe this is really happening."

"Believe it. You made it happen, and I'm so proud of you."

He smiled, leading me towards the doors. "Come with me. Let me show you what I've been working on."

THE END

THANK YOU

Thank you so much for reading JJ and Killian's story! Are you interested in reading more from some of the other characters? Check out the following:

Collided (Cole & Huxley)

Blindsided (Liam & Noah)

Sidelined (Ander & Elliot)

You can also find Niccolò and Bennett's story in the Hit Me With Your Best Shot anthology

If you want to know what's coming next, sign up to my newsletter for updates or come and find me on Facebook or Instagram. Check out all my links at https://linktr.ee/authorbeccasteele

Feel free to send me your thoughts, and reviews are always very appreciated 🖤

Becca xoxo

ACKNOWLEDGMENTS

JJ came into my life back in 2021 when I was writing *The Bonds We Break*, and I instantly knew he was going to be someone special. He kept appearing in my books and asking me for his own story, and after helping his friends out with their love lives, he finally got his well-deserved HEA with his very own doctor, Killian. I fell in love with their story, and I'm so happy they found each other.

So, with that being said, I need to thank a few people! First of all, thank you to Amy S for being JJ's biggest cheerleader and for your dance knowledge. Speaking of dance, thank you to the SaL choreo team for your valuable insight regarding studying for your dance degrees and teaching dance classes at the same time, as well as various other dance-related things that found their way into the story. I suppose I should also thank Andy (not that he will ever read this) for answering my random and weirdly specific questions about his experience as a uni lecturer.

I want to say thank you as always to Claudia and Jenny for your support and awesomeness, and to Amy V and Jenny for all your insight and feedback. You are so appreciated, and Ignited wouldn't be the same without you! Sandra and Rumi—thank you for making Ignited sparkle! Literally, in JJ's case. Thank you to my amazing Patreon readers, my blogger and ARC teams, Jen, Wordsmith, &

GRR, and to the book community—I love and appreciate all the reads, reviews, recommendations, promo, edits etc.

Finally, thank you so much for taking the time to pick up this book and read JJ and Killian's story. LSU will be back!

And one day, Sid will get his very own HEA.

Becca xoxo

LSU Series

(M/M college romance)

Collided

Blindsided

Sidelined

*Unwrapped (festive spin-off novella)**

Ignited

Gods of Hatherley Hall Series

(M/F academy romance)

Cruel Crypts

The Four Series

(M/F college suspense romance)

The Lies We Tell

The Secrets We Hide

The Havoc We Wreak

*A Cavendish Christmas (festive short story)**

The Fight In Us

The Bonds We Break

The Darkness In You

Alstone High Standalones

(new adult high school romance)

Trick Me Twice (M/F)

Cross the Line (M/M)

*In a Week (M/F short story)**

Savage Rivals (M/M)

London Players Series

(M/F rugby romance)

The Offer

London Suits Series

(M/F office romance)

The Deal

The Truce

*The Wish (a festive short story)**

Other Standalones

Cirque des Masques (M/M dark circus romance)

Reckless (M/M soccer romance)

*Mayhem (M/F Four series dark spinoff)**

*Heatwave (M/F summer short story)**

*After Dark (M/M/M Cirque des Masques short spinoff)**

Snowbound (M/F festive short story - Patreon exclusive)

Boneyard Kings Series (with C. Lymari)

(RH/why-choose college suspense romance)

Merciless Kings

Vicious Queen

Ruthless Kingdom

Box Sets

Caiden & Winter trilogy (M/F)

(*The Four series books 1-3*)

*starred books (plus bonus scenes) are available as free downloads
from https://authorbeccasteele.com*

**Key - M/F = Male/Female romance*

M/M = Male/Male romance

RH = Reverse Harem/why-choose (one woman & 3+ men) romance

ABOUT THE AUTHOR

Becca Steele is a USA Today and Wall Street Journal bestselling romance author. She currently lives in the south of England with a whole horde of characters that reside inside her head.

When she's not writing, you can find her reading or watching Netflix, usually with a glass of wine in hand. Failing that, she'll be online hunting for memes or making her 500th Spotify playlist.

Join Becca's Facebook reader group Becca's Book Bar, sign up to her mailing list, check out her Patreon, or find her via the following links:

facebook.com/authorbeccasteele

instagram.com/authorbeccasteele

bookbub.com/profile/becca-steele

goodreads.com/authorbeccasteele

patreon.com/authorbeccasteele

amazon.com/stores/Becca-Steele/author/B07WT6GWB2

www.ingramcontent.com/pod-product-compliance
Lightning Source LLC
Chambersburg PA
CBHW051254210726
48287CB00002B/492